Other Side of Yesterday

Other Side of Yesterday

A Novel by

Linda St. John

DDP

Divine Destiny Publishing

DDP
Divine Destiny Publishing

Copyright Linda St. John, 2019
All rights reserved

PUBLISHER'S NOTE

This is a work of fiction. All events and characters in this story are solely the product of the author's imagination. Any similarities between any characters and situations presented in this book to any individuals, living or dead, or actual places and situations are purely coincidental.

Cover artwork by Najwa Jai
Editing by Donna Shannon

Divine Destiny Publishing 2019
ISBN 978-1-7338950-4-0
Published in the United States

Dedication

To my beloved Mother, Lula M. Harris, who transitioned during the writing of this book.

Acknowledgement

All my love to my heart, my son Mayeer. Love to my heartbeats, granddaughters - Gabrielle, Cherish and Baylee. My "tribe" - Paris, Debra, Charlene, Desiree, Beverly, Shannon, Cynthia love you all from the deepest part of my soul. My fellow amazing, brilliant writers – Antoine and Coco.

Deeply grateful for Najwa Jai's creative artistry in not only in the conceptual vision but execution of a fabulous book cover.

Thank you to my editor Donna Shannon, you're the best!

Author's Note

This is a work of fiction. All events and characters in this story are solely the product of the author's imagination. Any similarities between any characters and situations presented in this book to any individuals, living or dead, or actual places and situations are purely coincidental.

Chapter 1

Zina took a long drag off the blunt. As she titled her Afro- crowned head back in order to feel the full effect of the weed, her curly crown nodded to the soft music gently playing in the background. She was elated that marijuana legislation had just passed in California. *The medical marijuana card was a wonderful gift,* she thought as she smiled a sly smile, closed her eyes, and took another drag. In a foggy daze, Zina blew circles of smoke. Her mind drifted to a painful place as the memories pulled her heartstrings.

Pushing feelings aside, she continued to numb the pain, if only temporarily. She was annoyed by the ringing cell phone interrupting her high and thoughts.

"Hello!" she answered curtly.

"Whew, what's up with that tone?" the smooth bass voice asked. A smile crept across her perfectly shaped pale pink lips.

"Hey, baby," she cooed into the phone.

"Queen, what's with the tone?" he asked again.

"No reason, just thinking about..."

"Baby, don't do that to yourself again...let it go. Listen, I'm doing a late night set and probably will be splitting around 2:30 a.m."

"That's cool. I'll just order Netflix."

"I know you're disappointed, babe, but I'll make it up to you— promise," he said with a smile in his voice.

All she could manage was a coy "okay."

"Later," he replied and hung up.

Zina crossed her cinnamon-colored legs and returned to euphoria, still feeling the effects of the weed. She wanted to enjoy the temporary escape. Nothing like avoiding your feelings. The music stopped. Now it was just her, alone with her thoughts and the loud silence. Needing to have noise, she selected the Jill Scott Woman CD on Spotify. She noticed her hands shaking just a little. She was nervous, anxious as the music began to play. She made her way over to the table and lit another blunt, unable to bear to feel....*anything*. Before long, Zina fell asleep.

She woke up around ten o'clock as hungry as a bear. Munchies. She arose and went into the kitchen. She heated up some peach cobbler in the microwave, topped it with some vanilla ice cream, and inhaled it until satisfied.

The noise sent her crashing back to sober thoughts. The CNN newscast sounded like gibberish for a brief second, as she sat on the retro red sofa checking her phone. She noticed a few missed calls and checked her voicemail messages.

"Hey girl, it's Lolo. Snowing here like crazy. Just wanted to hear your voice. Call me. Love you."

Her baby sister loved the ground she walked on. Zina missed her family so much, her heart ached. But she had to leave Chicago. This new journey was what her soul needed. There were a few more calls from prospective clients. She thanked God for living in a litigious society. Her paralegal business was booming, and she loved counting her coins.

Zina had attended Northwestern School of Law in Chicago, but dropped out after the tragedy and bounced, putting Chicago in her rearview mirror. She immediately pushed the thoughts of her hometown away, refusing to remember the painful place. She went to her bathroom, disrobed, and took a long hot shower. Afterward, she slipped into some sexy pajamas and fell into bed.

The sun peeking through the blinds was a nice surprise to a sleepy Zina, along with the smell of bacon, onions, and biscuits. She heard Donovan in the kitchen singing. His voice was somewhat raspy, but oh so sexy. She really was feeling this dude. They had been together for little over a year now, and he had proven to be a good man. Six feet one of fine chocolate, and delicious.

Donovan was a musician, an exceptional drummer. He breathed music; had rhythm in his veins. He also had a beautiful way about him—funky, smooth, a little offbeat, intelligent, sweet, and thoughtful.

Donovan had entered her life when she was vulnerable and lonely and her heart was somewhat closed, but he blindsided her. She was not looking for a relationship; she felt it was too soon after the tragedy. But the heart has a mind of its own. As a matter of fact, she had been minding her own business when he showed up from out of the blue. Maybe it was a guardian angel that sent him. She could not believe he was this good to her and did not want to rush things. He allowed her all the space she needed. Besides, he knew she was feeling him. It was in her smile and eyes that sparkled when he looked at her. It was the way her body melted when he touched her. Her body was a work of art, he loved every luscious curve. They fit like pieces of a puzzle. Donovan entered Zina's world at the appropriate time, and though her heart refused to accept it, her body—well, that was another story.

Donovan walked in with a breakfast tray complete with a single red rose. Ah, what joy! Her heart smiled.

"Hey, beautiful!"

She sat up in the bed and smiled. "Morning, sugah!"

The food smelled heavenly. He gently placed the tray in her lap and climbed onto the bed beside her as she ate the delicious meal. He gazed at her with a broad smile.

"Thank you, honey. You are so thoughtful...this is so good!"

"You're welcome"

"Donovan, did you eat?"

"Yes, I did."

"Here," she said shoving a forkful of country fried potatoes into his mouth.

He chewed.

"Baby, I'm good! I had some yogurt, toast and orange juice."

Donovan was from the South, born and bred. He was very close to his grandmother who resided with the family and cooked most of the meals. As a child, he stuck to her like glue. She was instrumental in shaping her young impressionable grandson. Grammy, as he affectionately called him, taught him to cook.

"Baby, you need to learn how to cook; can't depend on dem no- count women," he recalled her saying.

He took her advice to heart and learned how to cook. It was therapeutic for him. Every time he got into the kitchen, he felt not only her presence, but love. He had considered culinary school, but pushed the thought aside. Music was his love, his life. But whenever he had the opportunity to cook, he did, and the feedback was always great—full bellies, empty plates, and beautiful smiles. Zina cleaned her plate, smiled, and kissed him lovingly on the lips.

Donovan got dressed. He had to go to rehearsals while Zina lounged around in the bed for another hour or so. She was interrupted by the responsibility of defending clients. The demands of the profession were weighing on her, but she was hopelessly devoted to her clients and fought hard for their rights. She hated injustice of any kind.

Zina had to head downtown to file bankruptcy papers, then head over to another court to file documents to fight an unlawful eviction. Her beloved clients kept her hopping, but it was well worth it. She got up ready to fight the horrible Los Angeles traffic, cursing inwardly.

The knock on the door startled her.

"Who is it?"

"Hooker, open the door. It's me."

Me being Juan Carlos, her neighbor. Zina opened the door.

"Hey, come on in, but I'll be heading out shortly. What's going on?"

"Ms. Kitty's hair is falling out and I'm distraught!"

"What's wrong with her?" she asked, heading toward the bathroom to complete applying her makeup. Juan Carlos followed close on her heels.

"Girl, I just hate to see my baby like this. Took her to the vet and he said she has a nervous condition and gave me this medicine to put in her food. How in the hell does a kitty cat get a nervous condition?"

Zina listened as she kept applying makeup. Juan Carlos made his way to the mirror next to her and started applying a sheer pink lip gloss. Zina looked at him.

"That's way too much; you look like work! And don't be putting my lipstick on your crusty lips!"

Juan Carlos was an aging queen who was desperately trying to hold onto his youth, albeit unsuccessfully. A middle-aged Caucasian man with sharp features, bright dancing eyes, and a double chin. His hairline was escaping at a rapid speed and he had the audacity to sweep the thin strands in the front towards the side which refused to meet his hairline that was slowly running away. But he was stubborn and vain regarding superficial issues and his hair—or lack thereof— was a touchy subject.

Nevertheless, Juan Carlos was a joy, a gem who constantly looked out for Zina. He had been on disability for years due to a bad fall he suffered years ago; he'd had to undergo three back surgeries. He spent the best part of his days with his cat, Ms. Kitty, and frequently had sporadic brief relationships which left him sad, lonely, and broke-down. Their friendship developed soon after Zina relocated to West Hollywood from Chicago, Illinois. They both were nursing heartache at that time. Zina had suffered a terrible tragedy and Juan Carlos had just been dumped by the love of his life, Wade.

Juan Carlos had knocked on Zina's door to introduce himself, offering her a beautiful bamboo welcome-to-the-neighborhood plant. Zina made Pink Panties and they tried to drink their blues away, chatting into the wee hours of the night about their respective heartbreak. They've been close ever since. Juan Carlos loved Ms. Kitty, his companion when the nights got longer and lonelier. He would be lost without that cat.

"Honey, don't worry about your little raggedy cat. Ms. Kitty will bounce back, you'll see," Zina said, injecting humor to deflect a sad moment.

Juan Carlos smiled and started applying mascara.

"Get out of my makeup!" Zina snapped.

Juan Carlos jumped, smiled, and shimmied his way toward the front door, picking up Ms. Kitty.

"Yeah, baby, let's go home." he purred.

Chapter 2

Zina ran outside into the waiting embrace of the City of Angels. The sun smiled as she hurried in and out of the glorious, sunny day, rushing to file papers in separate courthouses. She made several calls to her clients, texting as well as emailing.

Zina obtained her degree in Criminal Justice and felt quite fulfilled. She loved being the Boss Lady, answering to no one. Arriving at home, she kicked off her shoes at the door and welcomed the quietness of the evening. The city noise and traffic had her nerves frayed. She refused to turn on the television or play music, instead just sit in the silence.

She checked her PayPal account and noticed the day's deposits into her account. She was satisfied with the balance. She worked hard and felt she had reasonable and fair fees. Besides, she was not in it for the coins.

She ran her hands through her curly fro, noting that she

had to check in with Omar, her hair stylist, soon. Alone with nothing but her thoughts, she became afraid. She selected Pieces of a Dream cd, closed her eyes, and tried to allow herself to get lost in the melody.

Zina couldn't quite achieve the peace she sought as sadness crept upon her, pulling her into a pit of despair. She reflected on what had transpired a few years earlier that shook her to the core. One tear began a lonely track down her face as she tried to push the tragedy from her memory, but to no avail.

She reached for her box and lit up a blunt, which was becoming a regular behavior pattern. Even Donovan had noticed and suggested she curtail smoking so much. Zina pushed the advice aside as she inhaled deeply and slowly blew out the smoke. Before long, she fell asleep.

She was awakened by her "boo thang" planting tender kisses on her lovely brown face. Smiling, she opened sleep-filled eyes and looked deeply into his.

"What's good, baby doll?"

"Hey, boo. What time is it?"

"3:30 AM. You must have been wiped out. What time did you get home?"

Zina rose up, fro flattened on the side.

"Around 6:30 PM. I'm really tired; busy all day."

"You want me to order in?"

Musicians, they are a special breed. He wants to eat at this hour, she thought.

"Well, I do have the munchies. What do you feel like?"

"Thai."

"Sounds good," Zina got up and made her way toward the bathroom. "I'm going to jump in the shower; are you going to order the food now or join me?"

The next morning, Juan Carlos came happily walking through her door with a Starbucks coffee in hand.

"Ms. Kitty is getting better, chica!"

"Ooh, my favorite! Thank you! Glad to hear about Ms. Kitty," she said reaching for the Starbucks.

Juan Carlos kneeled and let Ms. Kitty jump from his arm. Zina gave him the side eye...the last time Ms. Kitty was loose in her apartment, she peed behind the sofa.

"Don't trip, she used the bathroom before we came over," he said rolling his eyes.

"I saw the eye roll, hooker. Just make sure Ms. Kitty don't pee or you will get cut!" she laughed.

"Okay, okay, got it. Sit down and drink your coffee. Where you heading today?"

"Nowhere; lot of paperwork to complete."

Zina was relieved she didn't have to travel today. The LA traffic drained all the enzymes out of her body.

"What's up in your world?" she asked.

"Nada. Talked to Mother. She's coming over later."

"Is she okay?"

"Fine; bringing me some comida."

"Oh, what did she cook?"

"My favorite Tortilla Soup, and yes, you can have some." he purred.

Zina smiled and winked.

Unbeknownst to Zina, Juan Carlos did not care for Donovan, although he could not put his finger on why. There was something about this dude that troubled his soul.

Juan Carlos was the product of a wealthy Spanish father and Peruvian mother. It was a brief affair. His father is a diplomat for the Embassy of Spain. He comes from money. He met Luna at a political function. She fell madly in love with the handsome man.

He, on the other hand, was married with three children, all sons. Their affair lasted a few years. He bought her the apartment building in which Juan Carlos resides, and a house. He secretly supported her and the child for years. Luna and Juan Carlos were his second family until his wife discovered them. Although he continued to support them financially, they never saw him again. This left deep wounds on their souls. He and his mother were very close.

Juan Carlos is named after his grandfather. He blames himself for his dad's absence, spending his days and nights alone with his kitty and brief, empty one-night stands. Juan Carlos has issues with intimacy ever since he was used and dumped, so he involves himself in meaningless relationships where he does not have to commit to anyone long term.

Zina felt sorry for him but she never let on. Besides, he was a prideful man. His mother, on the other hand, was very outgoing, sociable, and active. She took dance classes. Luna had just buried her second husband. She seemed content, accepting the hand life had dealt her. She did not let regret rob her of living and just ran her fifth marathon.

Luna was an inspiration, too bad her beloved son was not as involved in life. It appeared to Zina that he was stuck, probably depressed and unable to get unstuck due to failed love affairs, an absent father, and the walls he erected. He lived a very isolated, lonely existence, with the exception of a few sporadic visits from ex- lovers getting money from him.

Juan Carlos was sad. He masked his misery with alcohol. There was many a day when he would drink until he passed out. Zina would be alerted by Ms. Kitty's cries. Juan Carlos had given Zina a key just in case. Good thing he did. Zina would put on a fresh, strong pot of coffee and run him a bath. Worked like a charm. Juan Carlos would be terribly embarrassed but grateful. Zina never asked questions. She let him have his dignity.

Zina worked through the pile of legal documents. She was able to file some paperwork electronically, but had to meet potential clients at Starbucks to sign documents.

Rushing in the mid-afternoon traffic, she made it on time for her appointment with Blair and Judy Smith.

It was a simple Chapter 7 bankruptcy. She arrived and was seated; they walked in shortly after her. Zina ordered herbal teas for them and explained the entire process, while offering encouraging words. Hearing about the process appeared to calm them, and the papers were signed as they continued chatting and drinking the herbal teas.

Zina bade them farewell. As soon as she entered the car, her thoughts were interrupted by the ringing cell phone. It was Marlo.

"Hey, baby girl!"

"Hello, Marlo."

"How are you, Z? Long time no hear from."

"Been busy. I'm good and you?"

"We are great!"

"What in the hell is going on in the Chi?"

"It's crazy, all the killings, but not against us. Mostly gang rivalries."

Marlo and her husband are both Chicago Police officers. Their father is a retired judge, and their mother was a stay-at-home mom.

Zina worried about them, realizing they must be under a great deal of strain with all the murders happening in Chicago. Marlo tried to reassure her, but Zina detected a tone in her voice—she was trying to sound brave, but Zina sensed nervousness.

"Please be careful, and tell brother-in-law, too."

"We will. Never leave the house without our vests and, of course, we are strapped. You also have to realize we don't live in the city. We're out here in Carol Stream, away from all the madness."

"Be that as it may, you still have to work in the city. Besides, a bullet don't have no name on it."

"True, but we're good, trust me."

Zina braced herself for the question she knew was coming. "You coming home for Thanksgiving?"

"Not sure. I'm super busy."

"Well, Dad and Mom would really like to see you. We all would."

Zina felt a tinge of sadness. It had been a while since she'd been in Chicago. The tragedy left her empty. She wasn't ready to visit those familiar places. She wanted to leave the hurt there in the Midwest, away from sunny and beautiful California. The empty silence was loud enough for Marlo to pick up the hint.

"Gotta go Z. Love you."

"Love you, too." Zina said, and blew her sister a kiss into the phone.

Chapter 3

*T*ears began to flow from her soft, brown eyes. Oh, how she missed Marlo and her brother Xavier. Pieces of her had remained in Chicago, but Zina had changed. She wasn't the same person today as she'd been in Chicago. She was carefree, spontaneous, and addicted in this season. In Chicago, she'd been in love, happy and responsible, doing all the right things that were instilled in her. She was in college, on the dean's list, and in love with the most wonderful man on the planet, Troy Blackwell. He was and would always be the love of her life, truly a gift from God. Her heart began to hurt as she revisited Troy's memory and the life they'd shared. It had been magical. A love story written by God. But tragedy stole him from her embrace, and as a result, Zina would never be the same again.

She missed her family, and felt disconnected at times, being far away from them. Xavier, her brother, was a high school teacher. He loved his job teaching high school English in Chicago's inner city. He felt he was making a difference in the lives of youth. She smiled thinking about her beloved brother. He was a good dude. His wife, Belinda, was a good soul also. She was a dental assistant. They had a good life and fit like pieces to a puzzle.

Zina felt a tinge of envy. She'd had the same magic with Troy; she missed him so. The deep pain in her soul was unimaginable, but the memories forced her to relive the tragedy over and over again. She ran away, craved new surroundings, a new life. She had to shed the old life with Troy. The thought of him—their favorite places in and around the city, their Hyde Park love den—too many painful memories.

Zina had run as far as the wind would take her. She ended up in Los Angeles, California, the City of Angels. How fitting. She needed angels to surround and protect her from all the pain and trauma she had endured. When love knocked on the door to her heart again in the form of a musician named Donovan, she had reservations as first. He was fine and sexy, a good man. She could not give all of herself to him because she did not want to be robbed of a good man again.

She was taking this relationship slow. Donovan was cool with it.

He didn't pressure her. Zina felt relieved to have him. He knew exactly when to give her the space she needed to sort out feelings. But on the other hand, he was there when she needed him to be. He complemented her; she did not need him to complete her. But there was an emptiness no one could satisfy, a place of despair that she would fall into and would have difficulty getting back to that place of joy.

It appeared foreign to her sometimes...joy. "Happy" was out of the question. She had the audacity to question God about why Troy had to leave. A comforting answer never came, so the next best thing Zina could do was suck on a blunt until the pain dissipated, at least for a while. Although weed offered a temporary escape from long- term pain, it was just a Band-Aid for the sore on her soul.

Zina journeyed to another place while under the influence, and seemed to have a moment of "happy" even if it was false. She could not be real, not yet, because it hurt too much, and quite frankly she was tired of hurting. She reached outside of herself for comfort, refusing to confront her feelings. The scars love left behind were still fresh. Thanks, Troy Blackwell. She felt a pang of guilt. It was not Troy's fault. It was love. She was so in love with Troy, she could not see straight. She was empty without him, love left her soul the day he...

Goodbye, love, forever.

No, not yet. Love was not through with her. Her heart smiled when she heard Donovan's smooth, sexy voice. She pushed the idea of love away. Away from her soul, most of all her heart. She did not want to succumb to it again. It was too soon to fall in love again.

Maybe she was confusing it with desiring companionship. But she was not looking for love or companionship.

Zina was cool. Why was love bothering her again so soon? But Donovan was patiently persistent in his pursuit. She felt they had more of a friendship than a romance; this is what she reasoned in her mind and heart. But the heart has a mind of its own. Zina did not have time to surrender to love. She was far from being completely over Troy. But here comes fine-ass Donovan saying all the right things at the right moments. Touching her body, mind, and soul in all the right places.

Is this some kind of a joke love is playing on me? Zina wondered. If so, she was not amused. The nerve of her heart to start pounding when she saw or heard Donovan. It really pissed her off to the tenth degree of pissivity. She needed to relax. As she sipped on some red wine, she felt tingling inside. Wine mellowed her out along with the blunt. She tasted the red juice as she licked her naked brown lips.

Juan Carlos had given her this wine; brought it all the way back from Napa Valley when he went on a wine tasting tour. It was really good and she was feeling no pain.

"You smoking a little too much weed, girl," Desiree stated.

Zina ignored her friend and blew smoke circles in her face just to annoy her.

Desiree waved the smoke out of her face.

"Mind yo' business and stay up out of mine."

"Just keeping it real and being your friend. Seems to me you are smoking more than usual. What's up with that?" Desiree asked with a concerned look on her pretty caramel face.

They had met at the beauty shop through their hair stylist, Omar, and hit if off instantly. Desiree was a beautiful caramel-colored woman with a killer body. She rocked beautiful honey-blond Sistah dreadlocks. She had big, soulful eyes, deep dimples, and a heart of gold. She was a petite lady with three children and a fine husband. Her husband had his own successful construction company. Desiree did not look a day over 45 years old, and was always getting hit on by younger men, which she hated.

"Nothing, I'm good," Zina answered.

"Doesn't appear that way. You need to go talk to somebody, join a grief support group or something. You cannot heal on your own, or continue to numb the pain by smoking weed. Baby, you got to confront the pain in order to process it." Desiree declared.

Zina felt the words resonate in her spirit. She knew Desiree was right, but she was not ready emotionally.

"I can't" was all she could whisper as she looked out through her living room window. A lonely tear began a track down her face. She did not bother to wipe it away. For what? It represented what she was feeling, sadness. You cannot erase sadness although she was trying her best to make it disappear, at least temporarily.

"I can look for a grief support group in this area, if you like."

Zina shook her head no.

Desiree decided not to pursue the matter.

"I miss him so much. I still can't believe he's gone." Desiree just listened to her friend, and felt her pain.

"Why did he leave me so soon? It's so unfair, and I'm angry."

Zina realized she was rambling and pulled back. She put out the blunt in the ashtray.

"You want something to eat?" she asked as she got up and headed toward the kitchen to heat up the Tortilla soup Juan Carlos had given her.

Desiree did feel a little hungry. "Yes!" she exclaimed.

Zina heated up the soup and served her friend.

"This is off the hook!" Desiree stated between bites.

"Yes, Juan Carlos' mom made it."

They ate in silence, licking the bowls clean. It was quiet and awkward, but Zina was thinking about Desiree's suggestion.

Chapter 4

*L*ate into the night, Donovan had returned from a set and picked up some bomb Chinese food. It was their farewell dinner.

"The meal was delicious! Thanks again, baby!"

He approached Zina, grabbed and squeezed her as he looked into her brown ocean-eyes.

"Really gonna miss you."

"I'm going to miss you too, Boo," she said, staring back at him.

He was headed on a world tour kicking off in Tokyo. He'd be gone for five months. Their relationship was secure; he trusted her, but Zina had reservations. She trusted him to a degree. Donovan was not aware of it, but Zina had painted him with the same brush that musicians are known for. Musicians on the road equals groupies, unlimited booty calls. She had heard the stories. She wanted to trust him, but her heart was unsure.

"I gave you the tour schedule, right?"

"Yes," she answered, avoiding his deep, penetrating eyes.

Zina knew if she looked at him for any period of time, she would begin to cry. She was struggling with this long absence. They had never been apart this long. How was she going to handle it? She felt she would manage. She would keep busy. Besides, this would be good for their relationship.

"Would you like some wine, babe?" she asked.

"Nah, I'm good."

"I'm going to run us a bath," she said, making her way to the bathroom.

After the long, luxurious bath, Donovan gave her a hot baby oil massage, and she fell asleep. Donovan left at 3:30 a.m. to catch his 5:00 a.m. flight. Zina was sleeping peacefully. He smiled looking at her cinnamon-brown leg and perfectly manicured toe peeking from the covers. He left a love note as he slipped off into the night.

Zina awakened to the sound of music coming from Juan Carlos' apartment. It was an old tune by Player...

"All day long wearing a mask of false bravado
Trying to keep up a smile that hides a tear
But as the sun goes down, I get that empty feeling again

How I wish to God that you were here"

She sat up. Her naked body felt heavenly. She discovered the note on the pillow from Donovan.

"Queen, thank you for allowing me to share your space. Although I will be away for a few months, I believe this tour will give both of us time. Time to think about one another, miss each other, and learn the value of what we have. You have taken up space not only in my heart, but my mind and soul. You are the perfect melody to my chorus, the beat of my heart, the rhythm of my rhyme. Miss you, and I'll be back so we can complete our love song. D."

She smiled as the tears began to flow down her brown cheeks. The note touched her heart in such a loving and special way. Zina missed him already but was still unwilling to completely give herself to him. This time apart would be good, she reasoned. She needed the space; maybe she'd check out some form of therapy so she could get to the root of her trust issues.

She made her way to the bathroom to wash her face and brush her teeth. Hungry, she decided to make breakfast. She whipped up some country fried potatoes with onions, sausage, wheat toast and fresh fruit. She didn't hear the music anymore. There was a knock on the door. No surprise.

"Good morning," Juan Carlos said, entering with Ms. Kitty under his arm.

"Hey, would you like some breakfast?"

"Honey, I smelled it; that's why I'm here!" he answered while maneuvering around the kitchen, making himself a plate.

"No coffee?" he asked.

"Feel free..."

Zina continued eating.

"Donovan left already?" Zina nodded her head yes.

Juan Carlos did not want to go any further, noticing the sadness on her face.

Zina was putting the last bite in her mouth when she received a text message from Donovan.

"Overlooking the vast ocean, thinking about your softness. Did you get my note?"

She replied, "Hello love, yes I did. Touched my soul and heart. Have a safe trip."

They continued their love dance of text messaging as Juan Carlos ate in silence.

Chapter 5

Zina was not digging the empty space. She hated being alone with her thoughts. It was a place she could not bear.

Besides that, she was out of marijuana, but it was raining and thundering; and she was not in the mood to get out in that rain. She did not have the energy, looking out of her living room window at the West Hollywood area. Her apartment sat on a small hill which afforded her a view of the City of Angels.

She peeked at the gray sky and dancing rain. It was as if she was looking into emptiness. The city was beautiful—the hills, buildings, and trees. However, she felt empty despite the city's busy traffic, snarled due to the rain, and people going about their daily lives. Zina wondered what all the hurrying was about, everyone dashing to and fro while she was *still*.

She was stuck in the other side of yesterday, with no clue how to wiggle out of yesterday to focus on today. Memories of

Troy arose. She hated when those memories tapped on her delicate shoulder. The past was always popping up. She wanted to disappear into her future, but the haunting memories would not allow her to do so. The reality of the tragic event shaped her today.

Today. Why couldn't she be present in today?

She sipped her green tea and once again was robbed of peace. Troy would not leave her alone as the last memory of him continued to flood her mind and soul. It was almost impossible to escape the pain. No matter how much weed she smoked, he still bothered her. No matter how she tried, she could not shake the other side of yesterday. Tears of frustration began to form and her heart turned upside down. She felt the weight of the pain. It was the other side that kept her tied to Troy. Donovan was her today but how could she live in both yesterday and today? Why was she so screwed up emotionally? Zina had to get out of her head and soon. She was going crazy!

Her phone rang, mercifully pulling her out of her thoughts. It was Desiree.

"Hello..."

"Why you sound so sad? You been crying?" Desiree queried. Zina sniffed.

"Oh, baby, I hate to see you going through these

changes."

"I'm okay. It's just one of those things that I gotta work through."

"Can't do it alone, Queen."

"Let's not have that recycled conversation again, please. Not today, Desiree."

"Okay, but I'm going to text you the information of the grief support meetings in your area. I have your permission to do that, right?"

"Yeah, yeah. You're going to worry me until I try one!"

"That's because I love you."

Zina smiled.

"Love you too. I know where your heart is, and thanks."

"You are so welcome. Talk to you soon."

"Bye."

As soon as she placed her phone down on the table, she received a notice from Donovan. Facetime.

"Hey, baby!"

He looked tired, but fine.

"Hello, love, how are you? You look tired, babe."

"I am. Just arrived in my room. We had five ovations, kept playing, and my arms are sore."

Donovan was an awesome drummer.

"Wish I were there to give you a baby oil massage."

They were both smiling. His smile was crooked, but sexy.

"Trying to grow a fro, I see."

"Yeah, you like?"

"I'm digging it. The goatee looks good to me, miss me?"

"You know I do."

"How have you been, Z?"

"Okay, today is kinda rough."

"Sorry, babe. I know the rain is a reminder of, well...you know."

She nodded her curly fro in agreement, and changed the subject.

"So, what type of souvenirs have you bought?"

"Nunya...wait and see!" he laughed.

They continued to chat and flirt for another twenty minutes, then Zina returned to the loneliness awaiting her. The rain was coming down, soft at first, then loud and hard. She was feeling the pounding of the raindrops. Why must she continue to revisit the tragic events? She tried to forget Chicago; wanted it to be a distant memory. But her family still resided there. The memories and pain still resided there. The tragedy still resided there. The stain of death still resided there.

The familiar knock on the door was that of Juan Carlos.

Zina opened it to behold a beautiful honey colored Maltese-poodle mix puppy.

"Take it, it's yours, my gift to you to help you not focus on Donovan's absence."

"Oooh, how adorable! Is it a boy or girl?"

"Boy. He's a rescue, about two months old. Let's pick a name." They went over several names, but nothing seemed to fit. "What about Bubba? Bradley?"

Those names did nothing for her. "Miles!"

"That's it! He's so cute, and that name fits."

"Can't wait to introduce him to D."

Miles started licking her while settling into her lap. Juan Carlos was silent, just smiling. The mention of Donovan made his skin crawl. Something was up with him, and he was very uneasy about it.

Desiree and Zina had decided to meet at Chin Chin's Sunset Plaza for an early dinner. The area was bustling with energy and excitement. Zina loved this area and chose to settle in West Hollywood. Her spot was old, quaint and cozy. This area was beautiful, with the Roxy right down the street, and lot of history right here on the Sunset Strip.

Zina waited patiently for her friend while checking out

the people running to and fro. Traffic was unbearable and the amount of time it took to get across town was increasing more and more. She despised it.

"Girl, I'm on La Cienega. This traffic is crazy; be there in a minute."

"Okay," was all Zina could muster.

Desiree was a stay-at-home mom, a wise soul, well-read, and could whip up some herbs for anything that ailed you. She was truly a dear friend and confidant. When she finally made it to the restaurant, Zina spotted her and waved her over.

"Sorry. This LA traffic really gets on my last nerve!" she exclaimed.

"I waited to order. You look good, I see you just had your locks tightened."

Desiree smiled.

"Yes, thanks girl. I'm so hungry!"

"Okay, let's order," Zina said, waving over the waitress.

"I'll have the Chinese Chicken Salad," Desiree stated, handing the menu back to the waitress.

"Chicken with broccoli for me please, thank you." Zina said.

"How you doing?" Desiree asked, concern on her face.

"Some days are good. Last week was the

...uh...anniversary, you know," Zina said, stammering to get the words out.

"Yes."

"Marlo called. They all want me home for Thanksgiving. Not sure if I can do that."

"Sometimes we have to confront our pain in order to overcome it."

"Well, that sounds good, but I'm not ready to confront it. It's still too soon and painful."

"Zina, you have to put some form of closure to it. Did you look at the list of grief support groups I texted you?"

"Yea. Thanks, Desiree."

"Are you going to go to one?" Zina hesitated.

"I'm not sure," she said as sadness enveloped her once again at the thought of attending a grief support group. "I'm just not comfortable discussing it openly with strangers."

"When will you be ready?"

Chapter 6

Zina was awakened by a horrific nightmare. The scene played over and over. That evening, she had prepared Troy's favorite meal and was awaiting his arrival. However, he never arrived.

Troy Blackwell had been killed leaving his agency.

It had been a frigid night in Chicago; the snow was piled up and stacked on the city streets. Troy was the CEO of a youth mentoring program in the heart of the inner city. He was a dedicated man, passionate in building young men up from the inside out. He had been in business for several years with the majority of his funding from grants and the city of Chicago; he also received support from private investors.

Unfortunately, the Russian Mafia were trying to strong-arm him into laundering their dirty money through his agency. Troy wasn't having it and stood his ground. They attempted all kind of tricks to change his mind such as paying off crooked politicians who attempted to delay funding.

Troy had been stressed, worried that the agency would not be able to stay afloat for another year. The funds were low; funding renewal was delayed, and he knew why. He tried to keep all of this madness from Zina, but she knew something was amiss. She couldn't help noticing his sleepless nights, the stress that was appearing on his handsome face, the few gray hairs springing up in his goatee, and the small bags forming under his beautiful brown eyes.

Her father, who was a retired judge, called in some favors to expedite the investigation of the murder. However, it went on for months. No killer was ever found, although the District Attorney's office narrowed it down to the Russian Mafia. They were known to be involved in a money laundering scheme and trying to strong arm local businesses. After Troy's murder, the other business owners surrendered to the Mafia.

Zina woke up sweating, breathing heavily. The memory of Troy in his casket was forever etched in her memory. She cried and screamed. Oh, how she missed him! They had been engaged to be married the following year. She felt cheated of happiness and it was hard for her to overcome the tragedy.

Zina rose to go to the kitchen and make Chamomile tea to calm her nerves. She sat at the kitchen table and silently wept while sipping her tea. Miles was looking at her with sad eyes.

"Hey, Miles, sorry I woke you."

He tried to jump into her lap; she helped him up and stroked him. Between the tea and love from Miles, she felt some comfort, albeit temporary. The rainy day was a reflection of how she felt inside. As the rain came down in a fury, Miles was shaking. She rubbed her furry friend, appreciating the company. The rain was rhythmic and melodic soothing to her troubled soul. Sitting in solitude as the rain danced outside her apartment, she wondered what was up with Juan Carlos. She had not seen him in a few days.

Although her phone was on vibrate, she was alerted when a text came through. She picked it up and smiled when she discovered it was from Donovan. He was leaving Tokyo for Germany and then France. It all sounded so exciting. She missed him terribly. As they engaged in their text love exchange, he was able to bring a smile to her face in spite of the pensive mood and funky weather. Too soon, though, their texting ended and she was sitting in silence again.

The thunder startled her and Miles. The puppy snuggled deeper into her lap as she continued to rub him. Lightning danced across the dark, gray sky as the rain came down in buckets. Zina was weary. She contemplated going home for

Thanksgiving, but was still apprehensive. The memories consumed her, and being back in Chicago would just reopen the deep and painful wounds. She had so many scars on her soul, and being back in the city where Troy was murdered would just add to her sorrow.

When her walls had begun to crumble, in walked a wonderful soul, Donovan. He was patient, kind, thoughtful, and gentle. Just what she needed, but she was unsure of where they were headed as a couple, and was in no hurry to get there. She was enjoying the journey. She was really feeling Donovan, but felt a snippet of guilt because it was so soon after Troy's murder. Or was it?

Zina decided to call Juan Carlos.

"Fabulous Central," he answered.

"Hello," she purred into the phone.

"Hey, this rain is working my very last nerve!"

"Haven't heard from you...is everything ok?"

"I'm fine. Had a late night, if you know what I mean..."

"Oh, okay. Well, it's been a few days."

"I'm just fabulous. Had a friend over and he was delicious...get my drift?" he said with a smile in his voice.

Zina laughed.

"Got it. Okay, Juan Carlos. Go 'head wit yo bad self!"

Zina hung up, still smiling and shaking her head. She thought about her friendship with Juan Carlos. He is white, single, and gay. She's African American, in a relationship and straight.

Their connection: heartbreak was the string that entwined them forever. Totally opposite lifestyles, but theirs was a unique friendship. Mutual respect. Besides, they liked each other. More importantly, they understood one another.

Juan Carlos owns the building and was the first person she met in West Hollywood upon her arrival from Chicago. They hit it off instantly, and he rented her the apartment without a credit check. He had a good feeling about her; she seemed honest. Juan Carlos showed her all the spots, and Zina fell in love with California. But Chicago still resided in her heart. Her family resided in Hyde Park on the south side of Chicago.

Memories of Chicago flooded her mind as she recalled the JA Grill, the Jamaican restaurant. Their food was literally jammin'. They lived an upper middle class life and were exposed to the best of everything, including vacations all over the world— Greece, Italy, Jerusalem. Her dad planned them every summer. Her family was well-rounded and cultured. Their house was filled with love and they were a tight knit family.

Her parents had migrated from the South in the early 50's, as did most African-American families. Employment opportunities were plentiful in the North for poor Blacks. Car factories, steel and mining companies, brickyards; these industries were thriving. People were able to provide for their families, buy homes and send their children to college. It was a prosperous season for African-American families. Zina's father ensured his children had an opportunity to attend college.

Zina loved law and decided to attend law school, but dropped out after a year. The tragedy had sucked all the air out of her. She could not continue in law school. Her parents were disappointed, but understood and supported her decision. She became a paralegal, and started her own very successful business. It was a difficult time, however, and her family allowed her space to process the tragedy. To their surprise, Zina relocated to California.

Chapter 7

She settled into the City of Angels and appeared to be moving her life forward. The marijuana was a Band-Aid to numb the internal pain. She had no coping skills to address the pain, but had refused the idea of therapy over and over again.

It was Saturday. Zina woke up to the sunlight peeking through the curtains. She turned over, awakening the honey-colored fur ball at the foot of the bed, Miles, her companion while Donovan was away on a world tour. God, she missed him. She was surprised he had aroused those feelings in her. She thought she was done with love. *No, not yet,* she smiled, thinking about her boo thang.

Donovan was delicious, just what she needed to make her feel alive again—that human touch, the belonging to someone special. She needed that. He was a gift just when she needed arms to hold her and comfort her in the lonely existence she had been slipping into.

West Hollywood embraced her. She got lost in the small city. And then one day he appeared in all of this wonderful splendor. She recalled their first meeting. Was it serendipity? Perhaps. She had just left the small bookstore with a stack of books when she ran into this gorgeous man.

She remembered it all so clearly. As she approached her car, she noticed him placing a note on the windshield. She clicked the remote alarm which startled him. He jumped and looked around, finding her watching him.

"What's going on?" she asked the handsome stranger.

"I accidently bumped your car and it appears there is a small scratch. I do apologize. I was just leaving you a note."

Zina rushed to look at the damage to her black Porsche Boxster. It was a very small scratch, but she admired the fact that he had the integrity to leave a note.

"My name is Donovan. Here is my information. I can take care of the damage, after all, your car is oh-so-fly." he smiled.

"I just bought it a couple of months ago. Thank you, Duncan."

"Donovan" he corrected her.

"Sorry, Donovan"

"And you are?"

"Zina."

She opened the door to place her books into the car. When they politely shook hands, Zina felt a spark, as did Donovan. She pulled away to deny the spark, but it was obvious.

"I can set up the appointment as soon you'd like; just call me and let me know what day works for you," he instructed her.

"Ok, I will do that, and thank you again. A lot of people would have just walked away without leaving a note. That's really decent of you," she said.

Donovan was flattered, taking note of how beautiful she was.

"Not a problem. So, Zina, just give me a call.

You can meet me at the shop and I'll take care of this."

"Okay, will do. Thank you again."

A week passed. They met at the shop on Melrose and La Brea. True to his word, Donovan was awaiting her arrival. While her car was being worked, on they walked over to Pink's for a quick bite. It was packed with tourists. Donovan was charming, polite and thoughtful. They ate and laughed. Time flew, and before she knew it, her car was ready. They walked back to the shop. Chapman pulled her car up and the bumper was like new.

"Chapman is the best in the city," Donovan bragged. "Wow, yes he is! Thank you so much, Donovan!"

"You're welcome, pretty lady."

Zina smiled. He had made her blush once again.

"Well, I must be going. Thanks for lunch."

"Z, would you have dinner with me?" he asked, smiling through perfectly stark white straight teeth.

Her lips formed to utter a no, but a yes slipped out.

Chapter 8

She felt renewed, but sad because a pang of guilt enveloped her. Troy. As much as she tried, it was difficult to push him out of her mind, body and soul. Her heart kept pulling her back into the other side of yesterday. But today, she wanted to focus on the now and not what was. It was painful.

The other side of yesterday kept her trapped in this emotional prison she was trying unsuccessfully to free herself from. It was hard, cold, and lonely. Zina suppressed those feelings, buried them deep within. The weed just put a Band-Aid on the pain, the internal battle of the inability to move forward. However, externally she was fighting another battle...addiction.

Zina was falling deeper and deeper into the hole of denial. The medical marijuana card was a drag. She had no serious health issues to warrant that card. It was just medicine to cover a deep-seated sore, the death of Troy Blackwell, her fiancé. That sore was crusty, painful, and she had no clue how to uncover that scab.

Manhattan Beach was packed on this particular sunny day, no surprise. The sun was beaming down on Zina's Afro crown as she bounced her way onto the hot sand, trying to find the perfect spot to chill. She had packed a few sandwiches, cold drinks and Eric Jerome Dickey's book "Blackbirds" in her tote bag. She needed to escape the noise of West Hollywood, which was small and tight. She felt like being free today.

She found a space in the middle of the beach, planted herself, opened the umbrella, secured it firmly, and laid back to people-watch and gaze upon the beautiful Pacific Ocean. The waves soothed her soul. She watched the surfers riding the waves with ease and skill. The water was bluish green. She wondered what God was thinking when He made the ocean. It was breathtaking. Several sailboats sprinkled about.

Zina had smoked a few blunts before leaving home and felt good. She reached into the tote and pulled out a cold Pepsi. She removed her top, revealing a hot pink bikini, but she kept her bottom covering on. She was wondering if she should go to Chicago for Thanksgiving. It was still a few months away, and she was feeling anxious already.

Zina fell asleep under the California sun. It was a peaceful rest. She awoke as the sun was descending, and for that she was thankful. It was perfect. The beach was no longer as crowded. It had cooled off considerably, and a breeze swept over her. The ocean waves had quieted, and Zina needed to have a conversation with God...

Zina felt disconnected and numb. The weed wasn't helping as much as usual. She was willing to go to Chicago, but emotionally she could not deal with what she'd have to face once touching the soil of Illinois. Why did she have to face the pain? Couldn't she avoid it?

But Marlo had a sense of urgency in her voice when informing her of how their parents were aging and getting frail. A pang of guilt swept across her. She wanted to crawl up into a ball inside of herself to hide from all the pain. Apparently, life was not going to allow her to continue to avoid the tragedy...

Thanksgiving in Chicago—her home, family—her heart sank as wondered how she'd be able to look upon the fabulous skyline and not remember those long walks along Lake Shore Drive with Troy. Would the familiar smell of Thanksgiving dinner trigger memories of the holidays she spent with him? How could she relive the intensity of that pain again? She was not strong enough to handle it; why couldn't her family understand? Why did Marlo continue to push her into making a decision she was unable to make?

Zina was torn. She missed her family on one hand, but on the other hand, was not ready to face yesterday. What was she to do? It was a lazy Saturday morning and Zina was dreading facing the day. She missed her boo. She and Donovan had chatted late last night via social media. He looked delicious! She was feeling a certain type of way about this man, but something inside was holding her back. She wanted to give her all to Donovan but was hesitant about releasing her heart. She was afraid, afraid to let her heart feel again. Afraid to love again.

To be alive and trust again was just too damn hard. She still had residual feelings for Troy, although he was deceased. Deceased. The word rang out like a scream. He still had her heart. Soul. She wanted to be free of the past. Why could she not free herself from this love trap? She was stuck. How could she get unstuck? Zina reached for a blunt, lit it, and smoked half of it. She felt better. She did not have to feel anything. Well, at least for a while.

Chapter 9

Rushing to Los Angeles Superior Court, Zina looked professional yet stunning in her black and white polka dot dress, black patent leather peep toe pumps, simple pearl necklace, earrings and bracelet. Her makeup was flawless and her curly fro was fly. As she entered the Court, she received the glances, some haters but mostly acknowledgements of her swag. She proceeded through the metal detectors and made her way up to the ninth floor.

Zina's paralegal game was on point. She never missed a deadline, and treated her clients like gold. If people only knew the secret pain she was dealing with. All the swag was just a drag. She was hurting, but she wore her mask with pride. The makeup, hair, and clothes were just a cover up of something deeper. The fact was that she had no more tears to shed for this heartache. She was fresh out of sorrow; had no more use for grief. However, she could not continue to push away the pain. It was killing her to wear the mask on a daily basis.

She just wanted to keep it one hundred.

Thank God for Desiree, Juan Carlos, and of course her boo thang, Donovan. They understood and loved her; for that, she was grateful. She fought for justice on behalf of her clients in filing the required paperwork, while the irony was that Troy's murder remained unsolved.

"She's still in the hospital, no change. Mom and Dad are worried sick,"

Marlo informed Zina. Her heart sank, and sadness enveloped her again as she relived the horror of her twin being shot. Nina was assisting Troy, and they had met that night to go over funding issues. Nina worked for the Community Development Department, which was awarded a large grant to develop programs for at-risk youth. Not only was she the grant writer, but she also knew other funding sources for Troy's business.

Troy was exiting the building when approached by two strangers dressed in all Black. He was forced back into the office. The next day, their bodies were found. Troy was deceased, but Nina was still breathing. It appeared the bullet went in and out of Nina. She had played dead so the assassins would not suspect that she was still alive. However, the bodies were discovered late, and she had lost consciousness.

When they were transported to the Cook County Hospital, Nina had a faint pulse. They worked on her for a while; she was in critical condition. She kept fading in and out. The family kept a vigil. This went on for days. Zina felt numb. She did not want to feel anymore, let alone process it as her best friend Desiree suggested. She reached for the blunt, lit it, inhaled and blew the smoke out. The smoke disappeared and seemed to take her memory of the pain with it. Just like yesterday, gone into thin air.

"I met someone," Juan Carlos purred.

Zina raised an eyebrow while she finished making Margaritas.

"Oh? Do tell."

"He's scrumptious! I don't want to say too much, not right now," he stated while rubbing Ms. Kitty, who was purring in his arms.

Zina placed the large pomegranate Margarita in front of him on the table. She then placed chips and salsa on the table. She watched as Juan Carlos dipped his large hands into the bowl with a chip and shoved it into his mouth.

"His name is Giovanni, and he is gorgeous—curly hair,

olive complexion, and the most beautiful hazel eyes! Whew!" Juan Carlos exclaimed fanning himself with bluish-gray fingernail polish.

Zina smiled.

"Sounds handsome, where did you met him?"

"I was doing some retail therapy and went into his salon for a haircut. Well, the rest is history. We connected that day and I really feel good about this relationship."

Zina had reservations. Juan Carlos fell in and out of relationships so frequently. He often was used by these so-called lovers. It was always about money. Juan Carlos hoped for meaningful hook-ups which only disappointed him time after time. He was a loving soul who was used by beautiful, gay boy-toys who often left him heartbroken and lonely, minus a few dollars. He was a wealthy man, but tried to keep it under wraps for fear of predators. However, once he'd had a couple of drinks, his lips got really loose.

Zina's heart went out to him. She was there to pick up the pieces when the dalliances ended, which was a regular occurrence. Juan Carlos kept going on and on about his new "love." Zina had tuned him out momentarily. She had heard the same song many times, though with different characters. She just smiled.

"He's a hair stylist?" Zina asked

"Yes, and he owns the salon. Finally found someone who can afford me," he chuckled.

"Where is his salon?"

"Beverly Hills, honey, on Rodeo, no doubt!"

Zina laughed at his comment.

"Well hallelujah!"

They both snickered. Miles jumped in Zina's lap, begging for attention. She stroked her furry friend.

"So, I see you two are getting along well!"

"Yes, Miles is my buddy. But I miss my baby."

"Really?" he said with a raised brow.

This news did not sit well with Juan Carlos, although he did not show his disappointment outwardly. Donovan was not the one for her; he just rubbed Juan Carlos the wrong way.

"Are you falling in love with him?"

A smiled appeared, although slight. She avoided his eyes and looked out of the window.

"I dig him a lot."

"Do you love him?" he asked again firmly.

Zina refused to answer, taking another sip of the Margarita.

"Ok, so you're not going to answer me?"

"No."

"Well!!" he said in a huff.

"Don't take it that way. I'm still trying to process Troy's death,. My emotions are all over the place. Please don't take it personally," she said, reaching over to touch his hand.

His warm eyes met hers.

"Oh, dear, I understand, sorry to push you like that," he replied, gently patting her hand.

"It's okay. I really have to come to terms with how I feel about Donovan without the guilt of my past. I'm so torn."

Juan Carlos nodded his head in agreement. They sat in the silence of the moment sipping the Margaritas and wondering what tomorrow would bring.

Chapter 10

*J*uan Carlos was busy with Giovanni. Their relationship seemed to be progressing. She silently hoped he found love this time. She felt sorry for him. She recognized the loneliness in his brown, vacant eyes because it was the same look reflected in her own eyes. Two souls connected by heartbreak. In this new season, she hoped love would return and resurrect their lonely empty hearts.

Troy Blackwell had been a quiet storm who entered her life unexpectedly. He was tall, fine, with sleepy deep-set brown eyes, big full lips, and a sexy smile framed by a goatee. He had soft, short, curly dreadlocks. He was medium-build wrapped in chocolate— smooth, easy, with a deep baritone voice. Troy was a proud man, not in a haughty manner, but in a deep and profound way. He had insight into the plight of his people and quietly fought to eradicate injustice toward Chicago's inner city youth.

Troy had felt compelled to invest in this demographic to build them from the inside out. He loved his community and took pride in his work. He poured himself into the young boys just like others had done for him growing up on the Southside of Chicago. He navigated his way through the jungle, side-stepping the Cabrini Green projects. He was focused and determined at a young age, witnessing the decay of his community, and the fire was lit in his soul to make a difference in the lives of Black youth.

Troy's mother was a hard working beautiful lady who had done the best she could raising her son and his sister Bailey. Their father died of cancer at the tender age of 35, leaving them devastated.

Troy's mother took action, getting her children involved in mentoring programs which planted a seed in Troy's impressionable mind. It was a sad time in their household. His father's death left a hole in their respective hearts. But, they moved forward and Mrs. Blackwell met a wonderful man a few years later. He was good to her children, a God-fearing man who was warm, gentle and kind. Troy noticed the way he treated his mother like a Queen. They married a year later. Troy saw the sparkle in his mother's eyes when his stepfather came home. She was really happy, and they moved to a better neighborhood.

Troy and Bailey continued to thrive; it appeared their stepfather had breathed new life into them. They both graduated high school and attended college. Bailey became a social worker and Troy worked for a non-profit agency before starting his own company. His stepfather assisted him financially as a silent investor. Troy was so grateful. His agency thrived and was very successful, making a lot of noise in the community. He received service awards for the work he was doing.

Troy was very proud but of his accomplishments in the community, but there was something missing...love. Then one day he happened upon a lovely lady on the L train. She was gorgeous, had an air about her, and smelled so good. He got a whiff of her perfume because she was seated right next to him. He inhaled her that day and never forgot the heavenly perfume.

That particular day on the L, a male passenger got a little aggressive because she refused to give him her number. Troy intervened and ole boy scurried away. He got the message loud and clear. Zina was relieved, and offered to buy Troy a cappuccino for rescuing her from the heathen. He blushed and agreed. They exited the L and made their way to a nearby Starbucks where they sat and chatted, and their souls connected on that beautiful spring day.

Troy and Zina became inseparable. After six intense months of dating, they moved into a lovely apartment in the Hyde Park section of Chicago. They fit like pieces to a puzzle, hearts entwined, and shared everything. On her birthday, they celebrated in style. He surprised her with a fabulous trip to Bermuda and popped the question. Zina was over the moon! Their respective families were happy as well. But the tragedy interrupted their bliss. It was sudden, heartbreaking, and knocked Zina off her feet.

The Russians had been causing a lot of problems in Chicago's inner city and they were under the microscope, but they were shrewd and ruthless in their dealings. They managed to go undetected for several years. However, the FBI probe was closing in on them. Troy kept all of this from Zina, who was busy planning their wedding, but the Russian mafia was coming down hard on him.

Then came that fateful night... Troy was locking up, and Nina was in the back heading towards the door when she heard Troy speaking to someone in a harsh tone. She closed the door to his office, locked it and overheard the man speak in a strange language. Russian. Troy had briefly told her they wanted to "invest" in his business but he had declined. However, they were aggressive and moving in on him. Nina did not fully understand what exactly that meant, and did not press the issue. In the office in the dark, she listened. She heard tussling, slaps, hits and furniture moving. They were fighting!

The Russian was unaware she was in the office frozen in fear. All of a sudden she heard a gunshot. She covered her mouth and started trembling, scared out of her mind, unable to move. Afterwards, she heard more movement, then suddenly the doorknob of the office door was turning! *Oh my God!* she thought as her breath left her body.

Then she heard footsteps moving away from the office door.

Relieved, Nina waited ten minutes, thought the coast was clear. With key in hand, she opened the door, walked out, and saw Troy lying in a pool of blood. She knew he was dead. Nina blinked back the tears and quietly exited through the back door which led to the alley. Unbeknownst to her, the assassins were in a Black SUV parked in the alley. Suddenly, they shined the headlights at the back door entrance, and then...complete darkness.

The murders made the Chicago Tribune headlines. They had no clues or DNA to trace who murdered Troy Blackwell and thought they had murdered his future sister-in-law. Zina had no words. Her world was snatched from up under her. Troy's funeral was huge. Zina was shocked that he was so well-regarded by so many people. His "boys" were the pallbearers. To make matters worse, it rained all day, as if heaven wept for the beloved Troy Blackwell.

Zina could not breathe, nor feel her heartbeat. She felt like a zombie. She was numb during the memorial service. Local news coverage, city council members, the mayor, community activists, family members, and friends were in attendance. It had been reported Nina was deceased; however, she was placed in witness protection custody. She had serious injuries and was rushed to the hospital. It had been a month. Everyone prayed for a full recovery. The doctor gave them a rope of hope when her condition went from critical to stable. That was good news; however, it still seemed bleak. Zina refused to discuss her twin sister; it was too painful, as her condition remained the same.

These are the memories that had left Zina consumed by pain, still unable to relax and really enjoy life and love again. She was still pondering whether she would go home for Thanksgiving. She would like to go see her twin sister, talk to her. Maybe she would go; she had to confront the pain sooner or later. A wave of fear washed over her, and she wished

Donovan was back to hold and comfort her.

"Howdy, stranger. Long time no see!" Zina said.

"I've been busy," Juan Carlos replied, smiling like a Cheshire cat.

He had on some nice charcoal gray slacks, a Black sweater, and had left Ms. Kitty home because she and Miles were having problems.

"You look great! The reason could only be Giovanni, right?"

"Yes, honey, I'm in love!"

For the one hundredth time, she thought to herself. "I hope this works out for you, dear."

"Giovanni had to go to New York on a business trip. I cannot wait to make that trip with him one day."

"So, you two are really getting close?"

"Yes, we are." he purred.

Giovanni Mancini was born and raised in New York. The seventh son of Italian immigrants, they had struggled to make ends meet. His father was a tailor while his mother was a homemaker. Times had been tough for the Mancini family. Giovanni was the creative soul of the family. He loved styling hair from an early age, and did his friends' hair in high school. After high school, he attended cosmetology school and excelled. He landed a job immediately upon receiving his license. He had a knack for hair, it came naturally. He was making a name for himself, not only in the beauty world, but also in the gay community.

Giovanni was a "pretty boy" who did not mind being kept by closeted older wealthy men. He was gaining a reputation and was well sought out due to being a good looking guy. He had intense hazel eyes that were mesmerizing, and he was very seductive. He liked being taken care of, but maintained a sense of independence by being a hair stylist.

Giovanni was also a user, manipulative and cunning. He had a sense of entitlement. He was self-absorbed and untrustworthy.

However, he was as charming as a snake and was making his rounds in the gay circuit. But that did not deter the suitors that were lined up--one of which was a wealthy middle-aged hedge fund manager, Ian. He had homes on both coasts, in Bridgeport, Connecticut as well as Beverly Hills, California; a private plane and all the other trappings of wealth. Giovanni sank his claws into Ian quickly, and Ian was hooked.

It did not matter that Ian was married with three grown children. Ian spoiled Giovanni rotten and Giovanni had no problem with being pampered with spa weekends, etc. Ian also gifted him with a classic Mercedes Benz for his birthday. Ian is also the "secret investor"

who purchased his salon in Beverly Hills. Ian was a very shrewd businessman. There were no legal ties. He covered his tracks, left no paper trail, and had the best attorneys money could buy. Ian came to the west coast twice a month to visit his lover. It was an "arrangement," and both understood and respected it. Giovanni was involved with others and Ian did not care as long as he made time for him.

All of this information was kept from Juan Carlos, of course. Giovanni was indifferent toward his new lover. He started asking for money, and Juan Carlos did not mind, taking him on shopping sprees for clothes and paying his credit card bills. In the meantime, Giovanni was stacking his money in a secret bank account. He was making plans to leave California when he had accumulated enough to live comfortably. Never mind the trail of broken hearts he would leave behind on both coasts. Juan Carlos would just be collateral damage.

Chapter 11

"You should go" Desiree told Zina as they talked about upcoming Thanksgiving holiday plans.

"Yes, I think I will. It's really been a difficult decision. I've been struggling with it for some time" Zina replied.

"I'm sure it's been tough. But look at the positive aspects—you'll get a chance to see your family."

Zina smiled and let out a big sigh. Desiree could sense the weight of the decision.

"How long will you be gone?"

"A few weeks."

"And when will your boo thang be back?"

"In late January. I'll be so glad to see him! I really miss him."

"Yeah, I hear you. So, you're really feeling a certain kinda way about him, huh?"

A smile crossed her nude lips.

"Yes. It was only after he went on tour that I realized it. Funny, huh?"

"Yea, real funny. You never miss your water 'til your well runs dry."

"Amen."

"Speaking of boo thang—girl, let me go. Gotta make dinner!"

"What's for dinner, girl?"

"Tacos!"

"Okay, Senorita! I'll talk to you before I leave for Chicago."

"Make sure you do!"

"Love you, Z."

"Love you back!"

Chapter 12

*T*he Russians assumed Nina was deceased. The Chicago Tribune reported her dead. The FBI and other law enforcement agencies placed her under witness protective custody since she could possibly identify who murdered Troy Blackwell. There was twenty-four-hour police protection at her hospital door. Zina arrived in Chicago on November 3rd. She became sad overlooking the magnificent Lake Shore skyline as the plane made its way to O'Hare International Airport. She had to choke back tears.

The sun was setting, which made for a glorious landing. She pulled out her compact to freshen her makeup. She was home. Her heart fluttered a bit. A flood of memories consumed her mind. The late night stop to White Castle after the club, or kicking it on the beach during the hot, humid summer months, or hanging out at the "Taste" every year. She savored all the delicious moments that framed her life. She relished the memories. The seasons of her young life growing up in this city would hold her heart forever.

She thought about visiting Troy's gravesite, but her heart felt heavy. Maybe not. It would be good to see a few of her childhood friends; she was sure Marlo had told them she would be here.

All at once, it appeared the seasons of her life just slipped away.

She felt a sense of nothingness. She felt alone.

Frightened. Abandoned. Zina had not brought her "weed," but was sure she could get something while visiting. Weed was her coping mechanism; her fake lover that offered brief escapes into numbness, allowing her to feel no pain. This lover was thoughtful in allowing her not to feel. But there was her other lover, Donovan. He was pulling at her heartstrings, causing her to feel. Her heart was full and she was slowly falling for this wonderful man, though she still felt a pang of guilt because it was so soon after Troy. She had to come to terms with this, but was conflicted and confused. Maybe she was only grateful for Donovan, and was confusing gratitude with love. How could that be? But her heart felt something other than gratitude. Love. She knew what it felt like. It was familiar to her—of that, she was sure. If only her mind would agree.

Marlo was a sight for sore eyes. Zina smiled while embracing her sister.

"I feel so special having Chicago's finest to collect me. Hey, baby girl!" she said, kissing her on the cheek.

Marlo squeezed her hard.

"Welcome home, Z. Missed you so much!"

Zina not only felt the loving embrace, but also her gun. "Thanks" was all she could muster.

"Why are you shaking? Are you nervous?"

"A little. Lots of memories. Let's not talk about me. You look great!"

Marlo smiled, locked her arm with her big sister, and placed her head on Zina's shoulder.

"Thanks. How was your flight?"

"Good."

They walked arm in arm through the crowded airport. Marlo had missed Zina terribly. They collected her luggage and were greeted by the chilly embrace of Chicago, Illinois. Soon they were shielded by Marlo's car, and she weaved in and out of the traffic like a pro as they headed toward their childhood home in Hyde Park.

"This is going to be the best Thanksgiving ever! So glad you came!"

Marlo squeezed Zina's hand.

Zina was taking in the beautiful city. She was afraid to speak Nina's name. She decided she would wait until she talked to her parents. The subject of their sister was hard on Marlo, too. "What's up with Xavier?"

"He and Belinda are great. Everyone is good. We're just hanging onto hope, believing Nina will wake up."

That statement crashed into a wall of silence all the way to their parents' home. When Marlo pulled up to the house, more feelings erupted within Zina's soul as she recalled her joyous childhood. They exited the car and made their way to the entrance. Her dad opened the door, and Zina melted into his arms. It was a long, loving embrace. Standing next to her father was her mom, a petite, beautiful lady with warm eyes. She squeezed her mother hard.

"Welcome home, baby" her mother whispered as she held Zina's face in her small, delicate hands as if to remember every beautiful feature of her firstborn.

"Mother, have you lost weight?"

"Well, a little dear. This sugah is bothering me," she said, laughing it off. Zina did not like how frail her mother looked.

Her father was quiet, smiling and just staring at her.

Moments later, her mother led them all into the elegant dining room.

"The house looks great, Mother! What did you cook? It smells heavenly!"

"Baby I made your favorite: oxtails, rice, black-eyed peas, and peach cobbler," she stated proudly.

"Oh my lord, really? "

Marlo and her dad disappeared. They went to bring in her luggage.

"You ready to eat, baby?"

"Yes!"

They had a wonderful meal and shared memories over dinner. Zina was glad she decided to come home. She noticed her dad was forgetful. Marlo and Xavier had failed to mention that. Just as they were finishing dessert, Xavier and Belinda arrived. They shared more warm embraces. Xavier announced they were expecting. Zina was happy for them! They looked happy.

It was so good to be home. Zina found herself on this side of tomorrow, and it felt strange. She was not accustomed to being present without the aid of her lover - marijuana. Feeling out of sorts, she was forced to face sober feelings. It felt odd. However, her father had a wine cellar and Zina took full advantage of it. Getting through today was difficult, but with a bottle of red wine and the fabulous dinner her mother prepared, Zina was feeling no pain.

The chill awakened her in the familiar surroundings of her old bedroom, which was now a guest room. She pulled the covers over her head, wishing she could stay in bed for a few more hours. She was tired due to the combination of jet lag and wine. She stretched out in the big bed and inhaled the aroma of fresh-brewed coffee summoning her to arise. The smells of home made her heart smile— sausage, grits and her Mother's homemade biscuits. The aroma alone made her toes curl.

Zina threw the covers back, put on her robe, and made her way to the bathroom. After washing her face and brushing her teeth, she floated downstairs.

"Good morning! How did you sleep?" her mother asked. "Good morning...great, Mama! I smell your biscuits," she said, searching for them.

Her mother opened the oven door to remove the biscuits. Zina's eyes grew large. Her father was just making his way into the kitchen.

"Good morning," he mumbled, shuffling his way over to the coffee maker and pouring himself a cup of coffee.

Zina and her mom said in unison, "Good morning!"

Zina reached into the cabinet for a plate, worked her way over to the stove, and piled on the food. She stuffed herself. Afterward, she could barely move.

Her mother sipped her coffee and smiled. She was glad to see her daughter enjoy the food. It warmed her heart that she was home. She had missed her so.

Zina lounged around after breakfast for another hour, chatting with her parents, catching them up on her life in California. She finally made her way to the bathroom to shower. Her first order of business today was to go see her twin, Nina.

Nina looked as if she was sleeping. Zina could see that she had lost some weight. She squeezed Nina's hand and stared at her. The room was dark. Nina was hooked up to machines that monitored her vital signs. Other than the constant noise of the machines, the silence was deafening. A lump formed in Zina's throat, and she swallowed hard.

"Hey girl, I'm here. I've missed you so much, and I'm sorry you got shot. I just need you to wake up. Please."

A lone tear rolled down her cheek.

"God, heal our sister! Please wake her up. We are not ready to let her go. She has so much more living to do."

Her father and mother were just outside chatting with the undercover officer. Zina rubbed her face gently and started crying. She felt some guilt, but knew it was not her fault. It was an unfortunate situation. She wept with her face buried next to her sister's body. It was a good cry, a cleansing that she really needed to release. She had cried for months over Troy; she'd grieved and was still mourning.

Two of her childhood friends, Cynthia and Sandra, came to collect her from her parents' home. They went to a Thai restaurant in downtown Chicago for lunch. The weather was still crisp and cool. Zina felt as if her blood had thinned out since the move to Cali.

Although she wore layers of clothing, she was still a bit chilly. Nonetheless, they had a great time catching up on each other's lives.

The hot, spicy Thai food heated her up from the inside out. Her friends looked great and seemed happy. Cynthia was a Nurse at Cook County Hospital, while Sandra had just opened her own real estate firm. It was so good to see them. They were happy she had moved on after the tragedy, but they had missed her. She had known them since junior high school; they were close like sisters. They had lived in the same neighborhood and shared their lives until Zina moved to Cali.

They were part of the fabric of her life, threads intimately entwined. She loved them, and they felt the same.

"Let's plan a trip for next year!" Cynthia suggested enthusiastically.

"Where to? I'm down!" Zina replied.

"Spain!"

"Oooh, sounds good to me! Spanish men are so fine!" Sandra exclaimed.

"Calm down, sis!" Cynthia said, laughing.

"Count me in; that would be kinda fly," Zina added. "Ole boy won't mind?" Cynthia inquired.

"No, he's not possessive at all. Gives me my space."

"Okay, we'll work on it!" Sandra decided.

The ladies finished lunch; they offered to take her to the cemetery. Zina was grateful. She could not bear to make that journey alone. It was a forty-five minute drive. The ladies attempted to make polite conversation, but it was awkward and Zina realized what they were up to. Her heart smiled. The long winding road to Troy's gravesite was met with sorrow, and her heart began to sink upon approaching the familiar place. Cynthia stopped the car at a slight incline. She and Sandra remained inside, while Zina got out and made her way to his gravesite. Nina's gravesite was on the opposite side of the cemetary in a private family mausoleum. She informed them that she would not be visiting Nina's gravesite today but would return with her siblings.

It was just as she remembered, and old memories and feelings resurfaced. She ran her beautifully manicured hand across his name.

God, she missed him so! She began pulling weeds up from around the bottom of his headstone. Zina looked out at the Chicago skyline. His resting place was on a hill with a view of home, Chicago. Troy had loved this city almost as much as he loved her. It was only fitting that he would have a view of the city he'd held in his heart.

Chapter 13

The following day, the family prepared Thanksgiving dinner. Her Mother appeared to come alive; her warm eyes were aglow. All of her children would be at the house—well, all but one. The silence was thick; everyone had Nina on their minds but seemed afraid to say her name without the flood of painful memories stealing their joy.

It had snowed the night before Thanksgiving, covering the city with a blanket of whiteness. It was extremely cold. Zina gazed out the window while reminiscing about how she loved the snow. The house was humming with love as the smells of Thanksgiving wafted throughout the two story home. Her father added more firewood to the fireplace in the living room while Marlo, Belinda and a few cousins were in the kitchen. Zina joined them and was immediately put to work.

The ladies worked furiously to have the meal prepared

by 5:00 p.m. More family members came through, and the ladies could hear the football arguments. Little children ran around the massive house.

Zina smiled as love wrapped its arms around her. Family. God she'd missed them so. The thread of happiness was sown into the fabric of these few days of Zina's visit. They were happy for this time of bliss although short-lived. Cousins Zina had not seen since she left Chicago came by. It was a wonderful reunion; her heart leaped.

Thanksgiving dinner was served, and it was fabulous. Afterward, Zina and Xavier went to visit Nina at the hospital. It was a sad ending to a joyful day, but Zina wanted to see her one last time before she returned to Los Angeles. They walked down the hallway to Nin's room. It was dark. The machines monitoring her vital signs were still buzzing.

Zina took a seat by her bed. She looked good, like she was just sleeping, same as before. Xavier went over to the window and looked out of it. He was having a hard time dealing with Nina's condition.

Zina grabbed Nina's hand and squeezed it. She laid her head near her twin's side and silently wept. Xavier was quiet as a lone tear made a track down his cocoa brown face. Zina did not want to let Nina's hand go. Her eyes were closed as she whispered a silent prayer to God. The pain was deep. Zina raised her head, wiped her tears and just stared at Nina. Xavier had his back to them just continued staring out the window. Zina leaned back in the chair. All of a sudden the machine began to get louder. Nina's heartbeat was louder. Nina coughed! Zina sprang to her feet, and Xavier looked around. Nina started moving her head very slowly and fluttering her eyes.

"Oh my God!" was all Zina could say.

Xavier was frozen watching this unfold. Finally, Nina opened her eyes, meeting the stunned gaze of her sister's eyes.

Chapter 14

That night, Donovan and Zina spent an hour on Facetime. He looked tired to her, but still handsome. He would be home next month. She was really feeling him, to her surprise. However, she was still wrestling with residual feelings for Troy. Perhaps she did need to go to therapy to work out her feelings. Desiree was a wise woman and she did listen to her friend. Zina had to find a way to sort out her complicated emotions. She could not continue to feel this way.

Zina remained in Chicago a few more weeks. Nina's miraculous recovery was the best Thanksgiving the family could have hoped for. They were all over the moon. However, the doctor informed them there was work to do in that she had to undergo physical therapy to work on her motor skills, her memory was sketchy, and she was working with a speech pathologist as well as other specialists to regain what she had lost while comatose. Zina took that news as a mere formality. She had her twin back!

"I really don't want to go back home, just got you back" Zina informed Nina over the burner phone. She had been whisked away to an undisclosed location.

"I know...your life...in Cali...I'll...be fine ..." Nina struggled to express her thoughts.

"Marlo is supposed to visit me in Cali next spring or summer for a visit. Wish you could come, too." Zina insisted.

Nina smiled.

"I'm aware it's impossible because of the witness protection program."

"Wish I...could," Nina said as her eyes began to tear.

"So glad you are getting better."

Tears began to flow from both sisters' eyes. Zina was so grateful for her sister's recovery. Her heart swelled inside, full of joy. It was a long goodbye. The silence was interrupted by Marlo's heavy footsteps coming up the stairs.

"Okay, Z let's go! You're going to miss your plane."

Zina arose from the window seat, blew a kiss into the phone and handed it to Marlo. Zina and Nina were fraternal twins who loved each other deeply. Nina had deep side dimples, beautiful wide set brown eyes with long lashes and perfect lips, along with flawless caramel skin and thick black hair. Zina sported a curly Afro, while Nina wore her hair straight. They both had nose piercings with small diamond stud nose rings. Marlo checked her watch.

"Call...call...when..." Nina tried to command.

"...as soon as she returns to Cali," Marlo said, finishing her sister's thought and hanging up.

The snow had blanketed the city for three straight days. Nina was still using a walker. She was tired, lost in her thoughts, when Special Agent Jones brought in a tray with some tea.

Perfect timing; she thought, it would warm up her bones. "Tea time!"

Just what the doctor ordered!

"Thank you." Nina said.

Special Agent Jones placed the tray down on the table. She poured Nina a cup, as well as one for herself. The tea did the trick. Nina felt warm inside.

Chapter 15

Zina slept through most of the flight back to Los Angeles, and awakened just as the plane was descending. It was dusk, and the sky painted with orange hues which gave the city a glorious setting.

Inside the airport, Zina was greeted by Desiree's warm smile and embrace.

"How was your trip?" Desiree asked.

"Wonderful, awesome!"

"Great; welcome back!"

It was a cool 65 degrees, and Zina was overdressed. They climbed in Desiree's ride and were immediately thrust into the Los Angeles traffic. She started removing layers of clothes and felt happy knowing the memories of this trip would forever be etched in her heart.

Back at home, Zina was met with another warm greeting. "Ooh, I missed you, Miles!" Zina petted her canine companion and he licked her. He was very excited, as evidenced by his furiously wagging tail.

"Did Juan Carlos take good care of my baby?" she purred.

"That little raggedy-ass dog kept messing with Ms. Kitty. I had to keep him in a separate room!"

Zina chuckled and continue lavishing Miles with affection.

"So happy you had a nice holiday with your family," Juan Carlos said snapping his big manly fingers.

Zina thought about it, and a smiled appeared as she realized she was on this side of today, and it felt good. She had shed the hurt, and was ready to embrace today. This side of today felt really good; there was no need for a crutch. The coping mechanism of marijuana did not serve her now; instead, she leaned on the bliss in the awakening of her twin.

Zina was "woke" today, and wanted to remain that way. Being in a state of unconsciousness was no way to live, but that was how she had managed to survive. Living in a fog had only left her confused. Asleep. Unconscious.

Today, she decided to confront life head-on.

Zina started by cleaning her house from top to bottom. When she came across her "stash," she decided to throw it away. She had been home for three weeks and had not had a blunt since before she left for Chicago. Now that she had cast off the pain, she had begun to accept Troy's death. Chicago was the door she'd had to walk through. The trip afforded her the opportunity to say a final goodbye to Troy. She would always have the memories stored in her heart. Her twin awakening from the coma was the beginning of the peace that had eluded her for so long. No more guilt or shame.

Donovan returned from his tour. A new chapter in their lives was opening, and she was in a good place emotionally. No longer trapped in the other side of yesterday. She was in the living room and, hearing him turn the key, rushed over to the door to greet him with the biggest hug her small frame could manage.

"Baby, you feel so good," he uttered, holding Zina in his wide embrace.

Donovan looked delicious. Zina hugged him tightly, planting kisses all over his face. He smiled and returned the affection. His six- foot frame seemed massive to her five-foot three-inch body. His arms swallowed her petite body while planting kisses on top of her curly fro.

"Welcome home, sugah," she whispered.

Miles came running into the room barking at the

stranger. "Who's this?"

"Miles, a gift from Juan Carlos. Isn't he adorable?"

Donovan started rubbing the puppy, and Miles warmed up to him.

"Juan Carlos thought it would cheer me up while you were gone."

"Did it?"

"It helped, but nothing takes the place of you, baby."

"Thanks, but now I have to share you with him. He might get jealous."

"Miles will be okay, right buddy?"

She reached for him and began lavishing him with affection.

"I just don't want *you* to get jealous," she said, winking at Donovan.

"Nah, I'm good."

He reached down and kissed her deeply and long.

Zina awakened to Donovan's deep stare. She smiled, wrapped in the afterglow of love. How she had missed him. He kissed her on her cute button nose. She frowned playfully.

"Good morning baby," she whispered.

"Morning, Queen. Why the frown?" he asked, studying her face.

Zina was trying to frame what she wanted to say without hurting his feelings.

"Is it my breath?" he asked.

He knew her so well. He cupped his hand, blew into it, and caught a whiff of his morning breath.

"Smells like three day old collard greens," she said, letting out a loud laugh and hiding beneath the covers.

Donovan laughed out loud and got up to go brush his teeth. Zina peeked out from he covers in order to steal a glance of her boo thang. The morning held a sweetness and Zina was wrapped up in it. Soon Donovan was in the kitchen preparing breakfast, and it smelled delightful.

While enjoying the smell of the breakfast she would soon enjoy eating, she heard a buzz and noticed it was his cell phone. She picked it up and saw that the number was unfamiliar—perhaps an international call. Curious she wondered who it was. Although it aroused her suspicion, she was not in the habit of checking his cell phone. That was not her style, but something about this felt strange.

Donovan was busy in the kitchen. She heard him singing and cooking. She dialed the number. The phone rang and rang, and finally went to voicemail.

"Hi, this is Kiyomi. Leave a message and I'll call you

back." Zina was stunned.

Donovan appeared in the frame of the door, smiling with plate in hand. Zina still had his cell phone in her hand, with a shocked look on her face.

"Who is Kiyomi?"

Chapter 16

Zina was livid. Her hand trembled and she glared at her lover with a hateful intensity. He swallowed hard. Her eyes were locked on his every movement. He stood frozen in the frame of the door holding her breakfast plate. Overtaken with anger at this betrayal, she threw his phone towards him. He had the good sense to duck as the phone flew past his head. It was so close he felt the breeze.

"Answer me!" she demanded. He looked surprised.

"Somebody I met in Japan...it was nothing, I um...uhh..."

"Did you sleep with her?" Zina asked, glaring at him.

He held his head down.

"She is just somebody I kicked it with."

"Kicked it? What does that mean? Either you slept with her or you didn't."

"No, I did not sleep with her," he insisted.

"You two did not engage in any type of sexual act?"

He knew what she meant, and all he could do was hold his head down.

"Get out!" Zina screamed.

Donovan turned on his heels, plate in hand and made his way back to the kitchen.

Zina laid back down and began to weep. She felt like someone had punched her in the stomach. It was difficult to breathe. How could he? This Kiyomi had to mean something to him, because he gave her his cell number. What's up with that?

Feeling betrayed and hurt, she decided to tuck the pain in her pocket, and save it for another day. After all, it was familiar, pain too deep for words. Zina reached into her nightstand next to the bed and pulled out her box. *Damn*, she said to herself as she remembered she threw her stash away. She got up, showered, threw on some sweats and made her way to the spot on Pico and La Brea.

Back at home, she fired one up, inhaled deeply, and exhaled. Her escape. Back at it, and she was feeling no pain.

"Don't call me anymore!" he screamed into the phone. Kiyomi smiled.

"You did not like me?"

"You heard what I said."

"Did your girlfriend get mad at you?"

"None of your business!"

"I was your girlfriend when you were here. Was I not?" she asked.

"No, we just kicked it, don't get it twisted K. It was just a brief thing," he said, trying to justify his behavior.

"Does your girlfriend know it was more than a brief thing? I stayed with you a few weeks."

"So, you served your purpose, that's it!" he shouted and hung up.

Donovan immediately blocked her telephone number. He could not figure out how she got his number; Tony, the bass guitar player, probably gave it to her. He felt a sense of shame. He was unable to summon up the courage to call Zina. He was busted, but it was just a brief, meaningless thing with Kiyomi. It meant nothing. He felt stupid. He'd had no intention of hurting Zina. How was he going to repair the damage?

Zina was exhausted as she turned the key to her apartment. She opened the door and stepped into a room full of roses. It was breathtaking! She was taken aback. Miles ran to her begging for love and attention, his tail wagging. What a joy to be greeted by his unconditional (and faithful) love after a tough day. The courts, traffic, it had been a very busy, hectic day, and his little face was soothing to her weary soul.

The flowers were overwhelming but Zina was not willing to let him back in. It had been two weeks since she threw him out. She was also refusing his calls. But the flowers did get her attention. She knew Juan Carlos allowed them into her apartment. She wasn't mad, though, and a smile crossed her face.

She poured a glass of wine, sat down, and lit a blunt to unwind from the hectic day. All around her living room were the most exquisite flowers in every color imaginable. Miles jumped up on her lap as she was exhaling smoke. Zina got lost in her thoughts. She missed Donovan, but was not ready to talk to him. She did not know where to begin to initiate a conversation; the wound was too fresh, the betrayal too new. It had blindsided her.

The knock on the door started her. She jumped up. It was Juan Carlos. She opened the door.

"Nothing says I'm sorry better than a thousand roses!"

"Hello to you, too!" Zina responded.

Juan Carlos flew into her apartment in all of his glory. He was in a good mood.

"So, sugah, what do you say?" Zina shook her head.

"Don't know. Not ready. Would you like some wine?"

"Just a tiny sip, por favor."

Zina disappeared into the kitchen and came back with a glass of wine.

"Gracias," he said as he reached for the wine.

Zina was not in the mood to explain her feelings. She wanted to push them aside for another day.

"Can't avoid him forever."

"I know."

Zina wanted that comment to end the conversation about D. "What's going on with you?" she asked.

"Giovanni and I are great! Everything is groovy," Juan Carlos said, and gulped down the wine.

"Can I have another?"

That disturbed Zina's soul. Something was amiss.

(

Chapter 17

ina awakened to a slight hangover. Too much wine. She turned over and checked the time on her phone. It was 9:30 am, and she heard music. Her eyes squinted through the sunlight peeking through her bedroom window.

> "Girl, you know I love you
> No matter what you do
> And I hope you understand me
> Every word I say is true
> 'Cause I love you
> Baby I'm thinking of you
> Trying to be more of a man for you
> And I don't have much riches
> But we gonna see it through
> 'Cause I love you"

Who the hell was bumping Lenny Williams this damn early in the morning? How rude! The music blared loudly, which made her headache throb even more.

She got up and peeped out of the window. There he stood, looking fine, leaning against his car. His shirt was ruffled, open to his navel. His hairy, toned chest sent chills down her body. His tight jeans hugged every delicious curve of his muscular body. *Lawd, give me strength!* she halfheartedly prayed.

Donovan. She rushed out the front door.

"Turn that music off! I have a splitting headache!" she demanded. smirk on his face.

Donovan did as he was told. Zina was irritated by the sexy "You look beautiful" he whispered.

"Did you like the flowers?" Zina stared at him in unbelief.

"I have a headache. Let's go inside."

He followed close on her heels. Miles greeted him. He'd missed the little mutt, and reached down to pet him. Zina headed for the kitchen to make coffee. Her head was banging.

"How have you been, Z?"

She looked at him without answering. "Would you like a cup of coffee?"

"Yes."

"I have a headache. What do you want, D?"

"Let me give you a massage, just neck and shoulders," he offered, making his way over toward her.

Zina's hands flew up in defense.

"I'm good. Once I get this coffee in me, I'll be fine."

Then there was an uncomfortable silence. The air was thick, tense. Zina was staring at the Keurig waiting patiently for it to stop brewing. She'd wanted to avoid this moment with Donovan, but she had invited him in. A part of her wanted to slap the taste out of his mouth, but the other part wanted to inhale his masculinity and feel his large, loving embrace.

She was torn emotionally. It seemed she was living in this familiar place of emotional vulnerability, and it was uncomfortable. Her emotions were raw and on edge. She felt pathetic. She noticed Donovan out of her peripheral vision as he shifted his weight from side to side. He was just as uncomfortable as she was. He cleared his throat and managed to push his question out again.

"Did you like the flowers?" Zina shot him a look.

"Yes."

All Zina could offer him in this moment was one-word answers.

Finally, the coffee finished brewing. She poured him a cup, and herself a cup. She placed her coffee on the breakfast nook, and he joined her on the opposite side.

She inhaled the coffee. It was heavenly. She closed her eyes and let the caffeine work its magic. Again, Donovan broke the silence.

"I miss you...do you miss me?"

Zina's heart flipped. Eyes still closed, she felt him looking at her with intensity and did not want to open her eyes. No answer. She kept sipping her coffee.

"Baby...I'm sorry I hurt you. Please forgive me."

Zina opened her eyes and looked at him. His eyes were sad and tired, as if he had aged. His eyes told the story.

"What are you sorry for? Getting caught?"

Her voice was laced with anger. Donovan's eyes held her gaze.

"Sorry I hurt you."

Tears began to fill her brown eyes. Donovan arose and went over to hold her as she wept in his arms. She felt his sorrow and love. Zina wanted to welcome him back into her life, but was fearful. Trust is earned. Why would she let him back in?

"I love you so much, Z. I hope you can forgive me."

He continued to hold her tightly. Zina did not want him to ever let her go.

Chapter 18

The Pacific Ocean offered a welcome escape for Zina's soul. The weather was perfect and she was feeling a little sad about the other day with Donovan. She was torn, confused, and still hurt about his betrayal. She had on a lemon yellow bikini that clung to her body and every delicious curve. She had on an oversized hat and Ray Ban retro sunglasses. She was looking quite glamorous. She found a spot and planted herself on a blanket, her toes felt delightful in the cool sand. As she gazed upon the ocean, a calmness came over her. The ocean had that effect on her. Zina felt a sense of peace watching the water come and go upon the shore. She wanted the ocean to swallow her so her problems would disappear along with the pain. What to do about D? That was the million dollar question. A part of her wanted to rip his head off, while the other part wanted to forgive him and pick up the pieces of her heart and place them in his hands...again.

She had trusted him; had no valid reason not to. But here she was on this side of today with a broken heart, and emotionally fragile.

She pulled out a wine cooler and drank until she felt a little buzz. She was escaping her feelings again, trying to numb the pain. Zina had smoked two blunts before she left home, so she was eeling somewhat lit. The sun kissed her skin as she stretched out underneath it, just wanting to enjoy the high. There was no need to think about Donovan's cheating ass...

"You loaned him *two hundred thousand dollars?*" Zina asked Juan Carlos incredulously.

"Yes, but it's okay. I believe in Giovanni and his product line. I looked at the financial projections, and it's all good."

"Did you make him sign a promissory note or something? That's a nice piece of change to just hand over. I mean, I just don't want you to get burned," she warned. "Furthermore, why didn't you consult me?"

"Because I knew you would have talked me out of it, and I was not trying to hear that."

"Well, your best interest is my concern. You sure this is a legitimate business?"

"Yes, Giovanni has given me all of the documents. It's

legit, and I do trust him."

"Okay, nuff said."

Zina was not convinced this business deal was on the up and up. She had a bad feeling in her spirit. Instinct. Juan Carlos had not even known Giovanni for a year; it had been six months at best. Sounded like a well-thought-out hustle to her, but she kept it to herself. Juan Carlos was petting Ms. Kitty, and she sensed by the look on his face that he was not in the mood to discuss the matter any further.

Donovan was relentless in his pursuit of Zina. The begging, calling, and leaving messages continued. Her birthday was in a couple of days, and she was planning on heading to San Francisco to hang out with her favorite cousin, Cat. She had to get away. She felt crowded. Donovan was getting on her very last nerve. She had wrapped up several filings for clients before clearing her calendar. This was a much needed getaway. She had started feeling like a caged animal, dealing with the demands of her career, Donovan practically stalking her, and Juan Carlos and his current drama. It was too much. She needed to just chill.

Zina was preparing a spicy, flavorful meal for a late dinner when the knock at the door startled her.

"Whew, girl, what are you cooking? The entire building

is lit!" Juan Carlos exclaimed.

Zina smiled.

"Curry chicken, jasmine rice and steamed veggies. Would you care to join me?"

"Why, yes!"

He scooted in, gently putting down Ms. Kitty, who was hissing at Miles. Miles ran around her sniffing.

"It seems like they are warming up to one another."

"Yes, Dinner is served!"

Zina scooped up a healthy plate for her pal. Juan Carlos eyes grew big as he poured the wine. They ate in silence as Ledisi soothed their souls.

"The meal is delicious! Thank you, Z."

A smile crossed her face as she placed the last bite in her mouth.

"Why, thank you!"

"So, what's going on with Donovan? Is he still on you?"

"Like a cheap suit, and it's getting on my *very last nerve*."

"What are you going to do?"

"Not really sure; I need more time."

Zina got up and started placing the dishes in the dishwasher. Her doorbell rang.

"I'll get it," Juan Carlos said, heading toward the door

with Miles and Ms. Kitty fast on his heels.

"Delivery for Ms. Zina."

Zina approached and signed for the package with a puzzled look on her face.

As she closed the door, Juan Carlos sat on the sofa, and Miles and Ms. Kitty sat at attention nearby. The plain box had no return address. Zina looked at it, remembering the anthrax mail scare, when people were afraid to open mail with no return address. *The mail is safe now,* she decided, and she opened the box. Inside was a beautifully decorated gift box with a card inside.

"Happy Birthday My Queen. I love every inch of you." Donovan.

Inside was a beautiful, very expensive diamond tennis bracelet, it was exquisite.

"Wow, it's lovely!" Zina exclaimed with eyes open as wide as physically possible.

Juan Carlos nodded his head in agreement.

"It is lovely. He paid a pretty penny for that, Z. The quality, and those appear to be white diamonds. Look at the cut."

Juan Carlos knew jewelry. He had family members who were in that industry with stores in a Downtown Los Angeles jewelry mart.

"He is making it hard for me to say no. How can I? But he has to understand the depth of my hurt, and throwing expensive gifts at me is not the answer!"

"Yeah girl, but those diamonds don't hurt! At least you'll look good!"

Zina let out a laugh, shaking her head. She picked up the phone to call Donovan.

"Hello..."

Juan Carlos was smiling while ear hustling at the same time.

"Thank you. It's exquisite; a lovely surprise."

Maybe, but I'm taking off in the morning for a week, yes, San Francisco. Ok, bye."

Chapter 19

The flight to San Francisco was not quite an hour, and according to the pilot, the weather was perfect. Cat was awaiting her arrival. It had been a little over a year since she last saw Zina, and she looked beautiful. Cat is six feet tall, shapely, caramel colored with light brown eyes, big full lips, and a smile that would embarrass the sun.

"Hey, baby!" Cat said with outstretched arms.

"Cat, thanks for the invite! So good to see you!" The ladies kissed and hugged one another. In the parking garage, they climbed into Cat's classy convertible powder-blue Mercedes Benz. The sun smiled down on them as the wind sang a song in Zina's curly fro. They chatted and laughed as Cat weaved her way in and out of the traffic. Zina took in the breathtaking scenery.

They arrived at Cat's house and Zina was shown to her

room. Zina settled in and began to relax. She was very glad to have this time away from L.A., away from Donovan's ability to bother her.

Cat resided in a Victorian-style house in the Haight-Ashbury section of San Francisco with small funky boutiques and bookstores. It was a hippie neighborhood, and Cat fit right it. She was a jazz singer—beautiful, tall, and could really *sang!* Her vocal range was the envy of the Bay Area. She had her own following and was rooted and grounded in the culture of the fabulous area.

Her house was warm, eclectic, inviting, and hugged every soul who crossed the threshold. The bay windows offered sweeping views of the Bay, Oakland, Oakland Hills, as well as the Golden Gate Bridge. The house was huge, tastefully decorated, and appeared to swallow her cousin. The charming five bedroom, five bathroom house was lovely. Cat and her first husband had purchased it twenty- five years ago. Over time, major improvements had been made.

Cat had a few people in and out at various times. Out of work musicians would stay until the next gig came along. Or she would open her home to a down-and-out relative. Cat was as cool as a breeze and delightful company. She invited Z to visit after hearing about the problems between her and

Donovan. It was a welcome escape.

Zina joined Cat in the living room where she was smoking a blunt and drinking some Hennessey. Zina joined her, and they caught up on family business.

"Baby, join me tonight for my set!" Cat ordered.

"I would be delighted!"

The Black Cat is an intimate spot known for awesome drinks. Cat's band had been playing there for a while and had developed a large following. An eclectic mix of people began to fill the seats. Zina, Cat's hubby, and two of their friends had a table in front. Cat's band began playing Street Life by Randy Crawford.

Cat entered dressed in a leopard jumpsuit with gold accessories. She grabbed the microphone, and the magic began.

"I play the street life
Because there's no place I can go
Street life It's the only life I know
Street life And there's a thousand cards to play
Street life Until you play your life away"

The band was tight as she sang, making eye contact with her audience, smiling and owning the moment. Cat had the entire joint in the palm of her hand as she rewarded their attention with her vocal skills.

They arrived back at Cat's house before sunrise, still feeling the vibes. Restless, they shared a brandy. Zina collapsed into bed at 4 a.m. When Zina awoke, it was noon and she could hear Cat downstairs chatting on the phone. The smell of coffee beckoned her. She made her way downstairs to the sitting room to join Cat, who was dressed in a beautiful dress with oversized earrings, dangling bracelets and perfectly applied makeup. Zina helped herself to the bagels and cream cheese and a big cup of coffee. Cat ended her call and turned her attention to Zina.

"Good morning, sugah," she said, smiling.

"Morning, Queen. Last night was wonderful! You are an awesome songstress; hard to believe you do not have a recording contract. Your band was tight!"

Cat smiled and with a dismissive hand.

"I don't need to be validated by a recording contract. I sing because it makes my soul happy. Money can't buy that, baby doll."

Zina loved her cousin. She was so free!

"Get dressed! We are going to spend the day in Sausalito!"

Zina smiled and finished her coffee, then hurried up the elegant staircase.

They caught the ferry to Sausalito. Zina picked up a few clothing items and jewelry along the Sausalito boardwalk, and they grabbed a mid-afternoon bite at a sidewalk cafe. The Bay area was just the medicine for her soul. She felt free, as if a heavy load had been lifted. The beauty of the area, and the change—albeit temporary— made her feel as if she had new fresh air in her smog-filled lungs.

Zina and Cat chatted and laughed through bites. They did some more boutique shopping, then headed back to Cat's house. It was a lovely day. The warmth of the California sun kissed her skin as if to bid her farewell. She was returning to Los Angeles Sunday evening. Sorrow gripped her spirit as she thought about the rat race she would be headed back to. The client appointments, and Donovan's worrisome ass!

The vacation did not offer Zina any resolution regarding the pieces of her relationship. She spent very little time dealing with it. She focused on her time with Cat, enjoying their time together, not entertain thoughts of him. However, she knew upon her return that he would continue applying pressure, and she was not looking forward to it.

Chapter 20

ack at home, she had barely placed her luggage in the bedroom when she heard Juan Carlos at the front door.

"Chica?"

Zina opened the door. He had Miles in his big arms, and he flew in with the air.

"Take your little bully dog! He's been a handful, upsetting Ms. Kitty! Glad you're back. How was your trip?"

Zina scooped Miles up and began lavishing attention upon him.

"Thank you for dog-sitting. Sorry to hear he gave you a hard time. The trip was fabulous!" she said, turning to speak to Miles.

"Miles, you're not a bully are you?" she cooed while still petting him.

"That dog is the devil!" Juan Carlos snarled, turning on

his heels and leaving.

Zina laughed as she tickled Miles.

Monday ushered in a busyness Zina was not ready for, as she was still in vacation mode. She was stuck on the 101 freeway when her thoughts were interrupted by her ringing phone. Donovan again.

Well, she had to face the music of uncertainty.

"Hello," she answered curtly.

"Welcome back...how was your trip?" He sounded so sexy, she hated his ass.

"Wonderful, much needed."

"Good. Have dinner with me, Z."

Silence.

"Z?"

"I'll let you know, Donovan."

"Okay, I won't press you, Have a beautiful day."

"Bye," she said dryly.

Zina did not expect him to ask her out. She secretly wanted to see him because she missed *them*. However, on the other hand, she was still hurt. That feeling resonated in her spirit though she was struggling to move beyond it. He always did or said something to throw her off. He was full of surprises. Sneaky bastard!

They had dinner at Thai Town in Hollywood. The food was delicious! Donovan sensed that Zina was very much guarded. He was quiet and pensive as he studied her intensely. Zina felt something different about him, but could not figure it out. They ate and made small talk. He finally spoke, he had exciting news.

"I got an offer to play with Toni Braxton on a six month tour in the United States."

"I love her! You are going to take the gig, right?" Donovan looked away.

"What's the matter?" she asked, confused.

"I need to be sure I have you before I go on the road. I want us to be right, baby. You have not given me any indication that you are considering taking me back. Can't leave to go on the road with this hanging over me, over us."

He looked sad. Zina felt a pang inside. She could not pinpoint the feeling, but she did feel something. The ball was in her court, but she was still unsure.

"I can't be sure about *you*, D...us...and you're going on tour."

He looked away with sorrow all over his face, knowing he was the source of the uncertainty.

"I wish I could convince you to take me back. What is it

that I can do to make you change your mind?"

"Trust is earned, and there has been a breach. It's hard for me to trust you again. Not sure if we can get back to us."

Donovan searched her eyes for a different sign, but there was none. He lowered his head. Guilt and shame enveloped him and he had a look of defeat on his handsome face. They finished their meal in silence.

As he drove her home, very little was said between them. He pulled up in front of her apartment, turned off the car and was silent in another awkward moment. Zina smiled.

"Would you like to come in?" Donovan's heart skipped a beat.

"Yes, of course."

He got out and opened the door for his Queen, leading her by the hand. Inside, the apartment brought back beautiful memories they shared. Miles woke up and ran to the door while the key was turning. Donovan sat down on the couch, watching her every move. Zina floated around the apartment. Miles, having received the usual affectionate attention from Zina, ran over to him while Zina disappeared into the bedroom.

She reappeared with a beautifully wrapped gift.

"You know I did not forget your birthday. Trying to be slick, inviting me out tonight," she said with a mix of sarcasm, humor, and sweetness.

A slight smile crossed her lovely face. Donovan smiled a sly smile, reaching for the gift. He was touched she remembered.

"Thank you, baby."

He planted a kiss on her cheek, and unwrapped the gift to find a book, "The Greatest Male Drummers of all time: Top 100." He ran his fingers across the book as he quietly glanced through the pages. It was a very thoughtful gift. He was flattered.

"I love it, thank you."

Zina smiled. She knew he would. She went into the kitchen and returned with two wine glasses and some wine.

She poured him a drink, and one for herself.

"Happy birthday....give the drummer some!" she said smiling. Donovan raised his glass with the same sly smile.

They finished the bottle of wine. Donovan was giving Zina a foot massage, she was in heaven. She did miss him, missed *them*, but her heart was still unsure. Did she love him? She felt something for this man, but she was afraid to trust him again. This temporary feeling was something that she could not pin her hopes on. Going on the road for six months. Nah. She could not bear the separation nor the uncertainty of him having another weak moment.

Donovan broke the silence.

"They want my answer in a week. What do you say, baby?"

Zina's heart wanted to say no, but her mouth said, "Yes, we can try again."

Donovan was over the moon. He grabbed her, held her tight, and planted her with kisses all over her face as he quietly sobbed. Zina's heart melted. Her body did not have a choice in the matter, and their love was explosive.

Chapter 21

*D*onovan was planted at her house for an entire week, making up for lost time. Zina loved the attention. He was kind, thoughtful, and doted on her endlessly. Zina was flattered. He signed the contract and would be leaving for New York in two weeks. This caused her some anxiety, although she tried to mask it. He promised to keep the lines of communication open, Facetime, texting. He was determined to regain her trust. Zina was impressed, but cautious.

Every night was filled with something new and exciting. She was beside herself with joy, but in the back of her mind, she replayed the betrayal over and over again. She had to get it out of her head!

Donovan frequently came home with a beautiful bouquet of flowers, skinning and grinning. He was happy to be back with Zina and he expressed it daily. He gave her massages, ran warm baths, cooked a few meals. He was spoiling her and she relished every moment.

Zina received a text from Juan Carlos. "Chica, que paso?"

"Hola..."

"Are you decent? Can I come over for a glass of wine? Miss you like crazy, Ms. Kitty too!"

"Sure, come through!"

The knock on the door startled Miles and Donovan. She ran to answer it; she did miss Juan Carlos.

He flew in with the hot air, with Ms. Kitty tucked in his masculine arm.

"Hello! I brought wine; care for a drink?" he asked batting his eyelashes. Zina chuckled. Donovan smiled politely.

"Hey man, how you doing?"

"Groovy, just groovy! Z, we missed you!" he said, blowing kisses in the air toward her.

"Missed you too! Come in, let me get some glasses."

"Something smells divine, what'cha cooking?"

"Donovan is making spaghetti, garlic toast, salad...care to join us?"

"Ms. Kitty and I don't mind if we do, huh baby?" he purred.

"Put her down, she's ok," Zina assured him.

"Where is that devil disguised as a dog, Miles?" he asked looking around.

"I have him in my bathroom; did not want to have to break up a fight."

"Good," he said, emptying his arm of the white cat. "Meow"

"She's probably looking for Miles," Zina suggested.

Juan Carlos disagreed.

"I don't think so."

"Have a seat and let's chat!"

Donovan was in the kitchen putting the final touches on his meal. Juan Carlos planted himself down on the sofa, lips pursed and raised eyebrow.

"Do tell, girlfriend!"

Zina smiled, shook her head. "D and I are going to try again."

"I *see*. You look good, happy...glad to hear it!"

"Well, what about you? How's Giovanni?"

"Haven't spoken to him in about a week. I don't know what's going on with him, but I will find out!"

Zina sensed something wasn't right.

"Trouble in paradise?"

"No, but he has been kinda distant for some reason."

Zina knew this story all too well. She had a feeling in the pit of her stomach that perhaps Juan Carlos had been beaten out of his paper again.

"Dinner is served!" Donovan announced.

The following day, Zina paid Juan Carlos a visit after work. He was surprised, Zina was still dressed in her business attire. This visit was out of the ordinary, and he was a little concerned.

"Well, to what do I owe the pleasure? Is everything okay?"

"Just checking on you. Heard from Giovanni yet?"

"No, chica, he has not returned my calls and he's not responding to my text messages."

Zina raised a brow. Juan Carlos was sipping on Cuervo tequila— normally a bad sign when relationships were heading in the wrong direction, but he seemed unbothered by recent events with Giovanni.

"This does not concern you in the least?"

"I'm cool. He will get back to me, I trust him."

With that, Zina decided not to pursue the matter any further. She politely smiled and changed the subject.

"D is leaving tomorrow."

Juan Carlos couldn't help but notice her voice was laced with sadness.

"How do you feel about that?"

"Uneasy, but these feelings will pass."

"Hope so, girlfriend. Want a drink?"

The day came when Donovan had to leave to join Toni Braxton's tour. It was a cloudy, gray—perfectly fit Zina's mood. She hated goodbyes; however, this was just a temporary separation. A long one, but temporary.

Donovan was quiet, feeling sad. However, this gig was important. They ate breakfast in silence. He would be gone for six months, just touring the states, with breaks in between. He was ready to purchase a ring for his girl. There was a quiet tension between them, but they pushed the uncomfortable air aside.

"Gonna miss you, baby, but I'll be here in between the tour breaks, ok?" he said as he strapped himself into her car.

"Ok" she sighed, fighting back the tears.

He grabbed her right hand and planted kisses on the palm of her delicate manicured hand. Zina's heart smiled. He knew just what to do to make her feel like she was the only woman on the planet.

She had a restless night, tossing and turning to the point

of even disturbing Miles. When she checked the phone, it was 2:30 am.

Donovan had landed at JFK Airport in New York. She closed her eyes and rolled over just as the phone rang. Donovan was calling. They had a brief chat on Facetime. She missed him. He looked good, sleepy but fine. He made her ass hurt. She smiled at that thought and shortly thereafter, fell into a peaceful rest.

Chapter 22

The California sun peeped through her curtains awakening her to a new day. She rolled over and saw that Miles was up.

"Hey, Miles!"

Zina arose and went into the bathroom with her faithful pup on her heels.

She was grateful for this special gift from Juan Carlos. She wanted to linger in bed, but did not have that luxury today because she had to meet a prospective client. Trapped in traffic on the 405 freeway, Zina was slightly irritated. Her phone rang. Her mood lightened when she saw it was Marlo. She had not spoken to her sister for a while, and smiled at the call coming in just in time to keep her irritation from turning into outright anger.

"Hey, baby girl!" she answered, her voice laced with excitement.

"Hi..."

Marlo's voice sounded strange.

"What's up? I don't like the sound in your voice. Is everything ok?"

Zina's heart raced.

Silence... She heard soft sobs. Her heart kept racing.

"It's Mother."

"Yes? What's wrong with Mother?"

"She had a....*stroke.*"

"But she's okay, right?"

"No...please come...it does not look good, Z."

Zina's heart sank as another blow blindsided and rendered her speechless.

Another pregnant pause.

"Z?"

"Yes," she whispered.

"Mother has other problems. She also has a staph infection."

"What?"

"Yes. She is really weak, incoherent at times."

"I'll be there."

The following day, Zina caught the redeye to Chicago. Xavier met her at the airport and they headed straight to the hospital. All visitors had to wear protective masks and gowns because of the bacterial infection. Their mother looked frail; her skin had a gray appearance. She looked as if she had aged years, rather than just the weeks since Zina's last visit.

"Mama?"

Zina began to stroke her salt and pepper hair, and kissed her forehead. She was hooked up to a heart monitor, with a blood pressure gadget on her fingertip and an IV running through her veins.

Zina wanted a blunt. She pulled herself together and tried to offer some comfort to her mother, who had a vacant look in her eyes. Zina attempted to make small talk.

"Hey Mama, how do you feel?"

Her voice was just above a whisper.

"Not good, baby. Whatcha doin' here?"

"I had to come check on my girl."

Her mother fell asleep. Marlo arrived shortly thereafter in full uniform, worry enveloping her pretty face. They hugged. Marlo squeezed her sister. They went out into the hospital waiting area and chatted.

"How are you?" Marlo shook her head.

"Just trying to wrap my head around this. It's all so sudden. Daddy seems lost, unsure what to do. I've been staying over there with him."

"Where's Xavier?"

"He went to the cafeteria."

"What's her doctor saying?"

"Not much. They are treating the infection. They say she had a subacute stroke. I spoke to her after she had it and she was talking gibberish; I couldn't understand her at all."

Tears began to fall, Zina held her sister as she wept in her arms.

The night air was cool and crisp, and the Chicago skyline along Lakeshore Drive was breathtaking. Zina felt numb and out of sorts. The vision of her mother hooked up to all those machines worried her. The ride to her parents' home seemed long. Marlo was quiet. She and Zina were together, but alone in their respective thoughts. The familiar Chicago streets flooded Zina's mind with childhood memories, family gatherings, and trips. Chicago was her home, but it felt strange on this side of today while yesterday continued to beckon her into its seductive grasp. She hated this sadness. They arrived at the house and hurried inside to escape the cold January air. The house was warm and cozy.

"Daddy?" Marlo called loudly to be sure he could hear her.

He appeared from the kitchen, shuffling his way toward them holding a cup of hot liquid.

"Hey, made me some hot tea. I'm cold. Zina, how was your trip, baby?"

Zina made her way towards her father, who appeared frail and lost.

"The flight was okay. Hey, Daddy, let's go sit in the living room."

Glad you're here," he replied.

Zina guided him toward the massive room with a warm fire burning. He smiled following her directions. Marlo disappeared while Zina got her father settled into his favorite chair. She sat across from him as they silently stared into the fireplace.

Marlo reappeared with wine glasses and some wine. Zina's soul leaped for joy.

"Just what the doctor ordered," Marlo said, handing her a glass.

Zina noticed she had changed out of her police uniform. As their father quietly sipped his tea, Zina noticed his hand trembling. She guzzled her wine immediately.

"Whoa, slow down girl!" her sister cautioned.

"Are you hungry? I cooked some baked chicken, greens,

mac and cheese, and salad." Marlo asked.

"Sounds good, yes."

The house was eerily quiet. The siblings moved about making small talk, avoiding discussing their Mother. It was as if it was too sacred. Their father wasn't saying much.

"I don't want nothin' to eat," he insisted.

Zina didn't want to accept that he wouldn't eat.

"You sure? You're not hungry?"

He shook his head, placed the mug on the kitchen counter, and made his way toward the stairs.

"I'm going to bed...tired," he stated.

They decided to let him be. They knew he was struggling with the sudden illness of his wife of fifty years.

Marlo's cell phone rang. It was Xavier. Zina noticed the look on her face as she hung up the phone.

"Mom's in ICU."

Chapter 23

There was no question that they would return to the hospital right away. It was very dark and freezing when the family arrived back at the hospital, having abandoned dinner to rush back and check on Mother. Entering two at a time, Zina observed the machines, the ventilator, the IV line, and the constant noise of the machines.

She went over to the bed and once again rubbed her mother's salt and pepper hair. She was attempting to memorize every detail of her face. The shock that she had suddenly taken a turn for the worse had hit the family hard. She wanted the memory of her mother still alive to be stronger and clearer than what she would see if...if... She couldn't bring herself to finish the thought.

Her mother's eyes had closed and she had slipped into a coma, totally unaware of their presence. This saddened Zina.

She touched her pecan-colored face, still beautiful, no hard lines or wrinkles.

Her mother had lovely skin. She was intubated; she looked very frail and helpless. Grief swirled around the room. Sadness covered Zina and her siblings like a second skin. Their faces told the story. They moved about in silence. The nurse informed them their mother was not in pain, but was heavily sedated.

Zina left the ICU and went to the hospital lobby to send text messages to Donovan, Desiree, and Juan Carlos. She felt out of sorts. She observed other family members in the lobby with the same look of sadness upon their faces.

As death loomed in the shadows. Zina could not fathom losing her beloved mother. It was a scary thought and she immediately pushed it out of her mind. She made her way to the entrance of the hospital and sat on the bench just inside the doors because it was freezing outside. With part of her focus on trying to stay warm, she didn't have to focus all of her attention on what was happening with her mother.

Zina felt empty inside. What would she do without her mother? How would her father exist in a world without his wife? She attempted to push those thoughts out of her mind. *It's cold. Pull that sleeve back down. Hold the neck of the coat closed tighter. Why didn't I bring a heavier scarf?* But thoughts of her mother kept invading her space. Oh, what wouldn't she do for a blunt right now!

Once Zina, Marlo, and Xavier felt sure their mother was not about to die that night, they made their way back to the house. The January air offered no comfort, just a wind chill that made Zina cold to the bone. They hurried out of the frigid weather into the warm embrace of home.

The fireplace was warm and glowing. Zina made hot chocolate as they sat around the fireplace. Daddy was fast asleep. Xavier, Marlo, and Zina sipped on the hot liquid. It soothed their souls. It was late and they were worn-out, but neither of them was ready to go to bed. They dealt with their mother's illness quietly, afraid to utter the obvious. Death was staring them in their respective faces. They knew it, but wanted to avoid the reality of how serious their mother's condition was.

The next morning, Zina prepared breakfast. They continued to move around each other like strangers. Their father was quiet, not reacting much to their attempts to lift his spirits.

"Daddy, you need to come to the hospital with us this afternoon. It will do you good to see her." Zina pleaded.

He just shook his head indicating "no" and continued

sipping on his coffee.

Xavier left for his house late in the night. Marlo was working but in constant contact with them. The house felt strange without Mother moving about, cooking, and laughing. It was like the soul of the house was gone. Her laughter was infectious, from the innermost part of her being. She was the common thread of the fabric of this family, and now it was unraveling. What were they going to do?

They gathered together again at the hospital, minus their father, to see their beloved mother once again. She was still in ICU at the University of Chicago Medical Center. There had been no change. It was difficult for Zina to watch her Mother. She stroked her hair; it was soft as cotton. She was on a ventilator. Her bright eyes were closed.

Zina wanted to scream, "Please don't leave me! I need you! I'm not ready to let you go!" However, the words refused to leave her mouth. She stayed with her mother for another twenty minutes, then decided to leave the ICU and go outside for some fresh air.

Outside, Zina sat in Marlo's car and turned on the radio to V103. She stared at the hospital, watching people come and go, waiting for her mother to walk out. She was feeling hopeless. She knew her mother was slowly slipping away. An old song by the Stylistics interrupted her thoughts.

"Late at night when all the world is safe within their dreams,

I walk the shadows

Late at night an empty feeling creeps within my soul,

I feel so lonely

So I go into the darkness of the night

All alone I walk the streets until I find

Someone who is just like me

Looking for some company

Children of the night."

The tears poured out of her beautiful brown eyes. Her soul ached as she wept in the car alone, with the song mirroring what she was feeling. Zina wanted to crawl inside of her grief and stay there. She knew she should find comfort in knowing her mother would soon transition from death to everlasting life, but she felt no comfort at all. She felt scared, alone and empty.

Days and days passed. Their mother was holding on, no better and no worse. One Sunday just after midnight, Zina received a call from her mother's physician.

"Hello..."

"Hello, I'm calling to speak to Zina, please."

"Speaking."

Her hand trembled holding the phone. This would not be good news.

"Hello, Zina, this is Dr. Saban calling from the hospital. Your mother took a sudden severe turn for the worse tonight, with the staph infection and several pulmonary embolisms."

"Blood clots?" Zina asked nervously.

"Yes...she went into full cardiac arrest. We attempted to resuscitate her, but to no avail. I'm terribly sorry, we tried to save her life, but she passed away."

Tears began to flow from Zina's eyes at a furious pace. The doctor's voice was low, full of compassion.

"God bless you, Dr. Saban. We know you took good care of our mother. Thank you."

"Thank you. Again, my deepest sympathy."

They hung up. This was not unexpected, but she just wasn't ready. She had to sit down. No, she had to lie down and try not to think. But all she could do was think, and the pain was stabbing her like a knife. Her heart was heavy; she put her face into the pillow and cried like a baby. It was 12:30 a.m.; she had to wake her father and siblings with this horrible news.

Chapter 24

*J*uan Carlos hung up the phone call with Zina. With a troubled heart, he worried about how she would be affected by her beloved mother's death. With Donovan away, she was going to need all the moral support he could offer. But he had Giovanni on his mind and was on a mission to get to the bottom of his shenanigans. Giovanni had left his life as quickly as he had entered it, and Juan Carlos was nervous about what the private investigator would uncover.

Ms. Kitty was perched in his arms as Juan Carlos stroked her to ease his anxiety. He got up, emptied his arms of his furry friend, and headed toward the kitchen to make strawberry margaritas. He was lonely; the liquor was a temporary fix for a long-term issue, and only masked his pain. He missed Zina and his heart went out to her and the family, but he was dealing with his own crisis.

By the time he finished drinking two margaritas, he was feeling no pain. He was preparing himself for the bad news about Giovanni, and needed the liquid courage to handle yet another heartache. He did not know how much more he could take with all of the young lovers who just used and abused him.

The sadness snuck up on him, tapped him on his broad shoulders. Loneliness ate away at his soul. The young pretty boys who cruised the clubs spotted him a mile away. Word on the street was he was paid and lonely. He threw himself pity parties on the regular and was weary of the same old recycled crap. He knew he had to make some changes, but did not know where to start.

With the P.I.'s report, reality smacked and sucker-punched Juan Carlos in his gut. Giovanni was a professional, his lover/sponsor a wealthy closeted hedge fund manager. Juan Carlos was livid! He had been used again and felt enraged. He had invested a significant amount of money in Giovanni's business, only to determine he had been used and tossed aside like a raggedy old dishtowel.

Eventually, he got a call from the P.I. His face turned red as he listened to the P.I. delivering this news by phone. He paid the investigator ten thousand dollars, but it was worth every cent. He had been unable to locate Giovanni; he had disappeared from Beverly Hills as well as New York. The private investigator's leads were cold.

The news frustrated Juan Carlos; he wanted justice. This was not the outcome he was hoping for. He was out of a great deal of money. His pride was injured and he felt foolish.

Zina and her siblings made all of the funeral arrangements and everything went smoothly. The sky was clear and the weather was cold as the white limousine pulled up. The family walked hand-in- hand to the limo and rode silently to the church in Hyde Park where the children were raised, just a few blocks away from the house. Just seeing it brought back a flood of memories.

Nina was still under the witness protection program in an undisclosed location. The family was seated in the front pew. They all viewed Mother's lifeless body. She seemed to be just sleeping; there was a slight smile on her thin lips. The mortuary had done a wonderful job. She looked lovely in her white dress and beige faux fur jacket. Xavier had selected a beautiful casket. Flowers and plants surrounded the altar.

The celebration of life was filled with love as the minister spoke so lovingly of their beloved mother. She had been a member of the church for thirty years. This church was her family's foundation, a rock in the community. What was Daddy going to do now? What was Zina going to do without her Mama? A huge void enveloped her like she was being sucked down a dark hole.

It was difficult, but they got through it. Back at home, their father was beside himself. The family house seemed to swallow his tall, thin frame. Relatives came by with food, offering assistance as well as moral support. The house was full of warmth and love, just as their mother would have wanted it.

Zina left Chicago empty and sad. She cried daily. Her mother's sudden death had left a huge void in her life. She was unable to wrap her mind around not ever speaking with her again nor seeing her when she went home. She drank a bottle of wine almost every night to numb the pain. It appeared weed and wine were her only coping mechanisms. She was unaware that she was standing at the door to the black hole of addiction.

She was reflective on the flight home. She arrived back in Los Angeles and made her way to the baggage claim area, then to her car, and was quickly met by the never-ending L. A. traffic. She arrived home at 10:00 p.m.

It was good to be back in the City of Angels, but she missed her family already. Home in Chicago would never be the same without her mother fluttering about. Daddy was going to be so lonely without her. Zina had no family in L. A. and was wondering if she should move back to Chicago. But she immediately dismissed that idea. A text from Donovan invaded her thoughts. He was in Atlanta and will be in San Francisco in three days. He told her he was going to fly down for one day to be with her, which brought a smile to her somber face. She missed him so much! That night, Zina was restless. She had so much on her mind, missing her beloved Mother. Memories of Donovan invaded her space again. She could not wait to see him.

Zina got up to make some Chamomile tea to relax her nerves. She decided to take another week off from work. Her clients were understanding; important legal documents that needed to be filed were referred to her assistant. Zina lingered in bed for another hour; she was tired. She checked her phone to discover Juan Carlos had left a message along with a few texts. He must have wanted to catch her up on the latest news.

She arose an hour later, showered, ran to Panera Bread for a bagel and cream cheese, and Starbucks for coffee. Ten minutes after she got back home, Juan Carlos was at her door.

"Hey, chica, welcome home—and take yo' raggedy bully dog!"

Zina knew his humor was an attempt to soften her grief.

She smiled and reached for Miles.

"Hey, sugah, did you miss me?" she cooed. Miles licked her hand, tail wagging.

"I missed you too!" she said, wrapping her arms around his little furry body.

"Was he a good boy?" she asked Juan Carlos.

"For a minute. Had to keep him away from Ms. Kitty again! He is a bully!"

"Aw, my baby is not a bully! He is so loveable!"

"Humpf! Like I said before, that dog is the devil!" he said laughing.

Zina laughed, still petting Miles.

"How ya doing, girl? Juan Carlos asked.

"Okay, but it's so hard."

"I understand. If you need anything, give me a holler."

"Thank you," she said, reaching out and touching his hand. "I appreciate you keeping Miles. Hope he wasn't a lot of trouble."

"Naw, he wasn't."

"Donovan will be in for the day. He has to fly back early in the morning."

"Good."

Juan Carlos brought her up to date on Giovanni. She

was not surprised, but did not say I told you so. She continued to listen. Suddenly, Zina heard keys in her front door and jumped up. It was her boo thang, and he was a sight for sore eyes. She ran into his arms and cried. Donovan comforted her.

"I'm so sorry, baby" he said, stroking her hair.

"Hey Juan Carlos, what's up?"

"Donovan, how are you?"

"I'm good. Thanks for keeping Miles."

"You're welcome. Well, I must go." Juan Carlos rose to go to his apartment.

"You don't have to rush off," Zina assured him.

"Yeah, man," Donovan added.

"No, really, I have to. I'll see you tomorrow. Have a lovely evening. Bye."

And he was out the door.

Donovan ordered Thai food from their favorite restaurant. As he left to go get the food, he received a telephone call. While in the courtyard of the apartment, he was chatting in a low voice. Juan Carlos' window was open and he overheard Donovan's conversation. Juan Carlos was surprised to hear Donovan speaking fluently in a foreign language. He recognized the language because he once had a Russian maid. *I wonder if Zina is aware of this. She never mentioned it to me!*

Chapter 25

*J*uan Carlos decided to make himself a drink. He wondered if he should tell Zina about Donovan's foreign language skills. Maybe not; he did not want to rock their love boat. Besides, she had just suffered a huge loss and he did not want to add any problems to her already full plate.

Juan Carlos poured the red drink into a glass. He decided to keep this bit of information to himself, but he felt more strongly now that something was just not right with this dude. Juan Carlos had had been having suspicions about Donovan for a while.

Zina and Donovan spent the day hugged up. He was very loving and supportive as she cried in his arms. They drank Margarita's and ate Thai food. Zina felt good; she had a little buzz. Donovan, on the other hand, sipped on his drink. He missed her and showed her tenderness.

Later, as Zina was sleeping peacefully, Donovan left her a note, kissed her on the cheek, and quickly left for the airport; he had to make his flight to San Francisco.

Zina awakened to the love note. His thoughtfulness made her heart smile. She arose and made her way to the kitchen to make coffee. Her phone rang; it was Marlo.

"Hey, girl..."

"Good morning, Zina, how you doing?"

"Not good."

"The tears started to flow from her eyes.

"I know," Marlo said.

"We are dealing with it, but it's difficult. Daddy looks so lost and sad."

"I can only imagine, in the house where they shared their lives."

"Xavier and I came over and have been really supportive, but we're kinda worried about him."

"What's going on?"

"He's not eating as much; just sits in his chair and stares out of the window."

"Well, he's mourning just like us, so that's nothing unusual."

"I know, I'm just concerned about his loss of appetite."

"Zina's mind wandered off with thoughts about her mother. She recalled one of her mom's favorite fragrances was Wind Song. When she went home for Thanksgiving, that scent was combined with Ben Gay as her mother was fighting arthritis. The memories awakened a sadness in her.

Juan Carlos was in a funk. He was reflecting upon his sad life. Raised in West Los Angeles, he and his mother resided in a yellow house. He recalls his father's visit and how there was little to no interaction with him. He was distant, aloof, and they had never really formed a father-son bond.

His mother waited on his father hand and foot, totally submissive to a man who considered her a mere afterthought. She was his "secret" and Juan Carlos bore the shame of their affair. His father would come by when he was in town and have sex with his mother while Juan Carlos would be in the next room playing with the new toys his father bought him. He heard his mother's screams and hated what his father must have been doing to her.

His father seemed brutish toward his mother, and for that Juan Carlos developed a hatred toward him. He was somewhat scarred by the experience he had lived through for years. He never mentioned anything to his mother because he was embarrassed by it, and besides, he was raised to stay in a child's place.

After his father's visit, his mother would be in bed for three to four days. She'd appear sad and depressed. He hated his father's visits and hated the yellow house. He was so happy when his mother sold it and they moved to Brentwood. Memories of that yellow house haunted Juan Carlos for years. His mother seemed to be relieved after the move.

The affair went on for years before his father's wife discovered it and forbade him to continue seeing his mother. However, his father continued to take care of them financially until Juan Carlos was of age, and then set up a trust fund for him which he continues to live on. His mother is financially secure as well. But the sadness enveloped Juan Carlos like a second skin when his father no longer came to visit his son. He was conflicted about his father; he did not have a "normal," happy relationship with his father, and vowed never to have children because he did not want his children to feel abandoned.

Juan Carlos had a problem with intimacy, thus the empty sexual hookups with young pretty boys. It was a lonely existence that left him feeling isolated and masking his pain with alcohol. Though scarred by the childhood experience, he refused therapy. He was in need of love but unable to form relationships with loving souls.

Instead, it was all about his "paper" and how much he would pay for the company of young opportunistic men.

Juan Carlos was miserable, and had been for quite some time. He hated the color yellow because reminded him of the house he was reared in and how terrible his father treated his mother.

Sunrise over West Hollywood was gorgeous on this Sunday morning as Zina slowly opened her sleepy brown eyes. She heard Miles' feet scampering across the hardwood floors. Her little pup made his way to his food. She heard a familiar song coming from Juan Carlos' direction.

> *"At first I was afraid, I was petrified*
> *Kept thinking I could never live without you by my side*
> *But then I spent so many nights thinking how you did me wrong*
> *And I grew strong..."*

Zina rolled over in her queen-size bed. She knew Juan Carlos had the blues, and she knew the source of his heartbreak, Giovanni. Whenever he was feeling a certain kind of way, she could tell by his choice of music. This was also her cue to go check on him. She never knew what condition she would find him in. Would he be passed out on the floor?

Would he be nursing a drink or popping a pill? She was nervous, but decided to get up and go check on him.

Zina sat up and stepped into her house slippers, made coffee, showered, slipped on sweatpants and a tee shirt, and combed out her curls. She carried a large thermal coffee to her friend. She tapped on the door. The music volume decreased and Juan Carlos peered out of the door. He looked horrible! Zina held the thermal cup.

"Morning, got coffee?"

He opened the door so she could step into his apartment. It reeked of liquor. Juan Carlos' hair was all over his head and in the middle was the bald spot he attempted unsuccessfully to cover up. His face was red, eyes swollen. Zina's heart melted. He'd had a rough night and it showed.

"Thanks, girl, just want I need. I have an awful headache."

The music stopped. Ms. Kitty was walking about looking lost.

Juan Carlos scooped her up. He drank the coffee and sat down on the sofa.

"Please sit," he waved his arm toward the loveseat.

Just then, he abruptly sat up. Ms. Kitty jumped from his masculine arms as he ran to the bathroom. Zina heard him vomiting. She was relieved she had not found him passed out on the floor. Throwing up she could handle. She heard the water running and his electric toothbrush. Shortly thereafter, he emerged from the bathroom looking better; his color had returned.

"Whew, what a night!"

"Feeling better?" she asked.

"Yes. Got trashed last night. Well, you know."

She knew all too well and shook her curly fro.

"You need anything?" she asked as she rose to leave. "I'm good, thanks girl!"

Chapter 26

They had been through this so many times. Zina never asked questions; she didn't want to pry. But she did wonder if she should mention that perhaps he might have a drinking problem. Juan Carlos drank a lot, frequently, much of it out of loneliness. But she had no room to judge him because she smoked weed to numb her pain. Their common thread.

Loneliness and pain were the emotions they refused to confront; however, the very issues they failed to confront were most likely what they needed to tackle in order to get free. Nonetheless, on this side of today, neither one had the courage to face their respective fears. Still stuck on the other side of yesterday. What a pair they were, emotionally stuck without a clue how to get unstuck. Trapped by heartache and grief. Juan Carlos craved to be loved but was emotionally unattached because of his childhood scars. Zina felt pangs of guilt because her sister was shot and almost died. She felt some responsibility for it and was unable to shed the guilt. Although no one blamed her for the tragedy, she reached for alcohol and weed to numb those feelings and allow her to run from what she felt.

Zina had relocated to remove herself from the guilt, but the wounds were still fresh and she could not numb herself enough. No matter how far she attempted to remove herself, the memories of that phone call constantly haunted her. Her twin was shot, and her fiancé was dead.

It was Zina who had convinced her twin to assist Troy. Her sister was shot several times and the assassin thought she was dead. Thank God she survived. But Troy lost his life. Zina was tormented by the memories of what they shared and how his life was cut short. The tragedy stuck in her soul. Troy and her beloved twin sister. Zina got lost in the memories. She felt like she was drowning in the thoughts of the life she once shared with Troy.

Her heart was fragile until Donovan showed up and caught her off guard. He was not what she was expecting, but he was good for her heart, which was slowly mending. This side of today was full of pain and sorrow for her as well as Juan Carlos, who appeared to be on the edge of a serious meltdown. No word from Giovanni; the private investigator's lead got cold but he was still on the job.

Zina returned home and busied herself with legal paperwork, scheduling, and other work-related matters. Her calendar was packed for the remainder of the month. She was sipping some wine and checking her mail when she froze in fear, having come to an envelope regarding the LSAT prep course. Zina had decided to return to law school. She had her sights on USC's School of Law, but she had to take the Law School Admission Test first.

Her mother's death had greatly impacted her. She felt her mother was disappointed that she did not complete law school. This was Zina's way of honoring her beloved mother. She would pursue International Law. Troy's death had left a scar on her soul and she wanted justice. What better way to achieve that than becoming a lawyer? Troy and her mother would be so proud.

Zina's heart smiled. This was something positive. Besides, she loved the law. Her sis would be excited once she revealed the news. Zina felt good for a change. It had been a long time since she felt proud of herself. Way too long. She was really feeling herself. But she had to mentally prepare for the LSAT, and that meant curtailing her weed usage, at least for a minute. Had to clear her head.

She was determined to get into USC to finish what she started back in Chicago. Her heart sank thinking about when she entered Northwestern School of Law. She was so excited at the time!

Tragedy robbed her of that joy. But on this side of today, she was ready to begin again. Ready to face the challenges of studying what she loved, the law. She looked forward to embracing the journey. For now, she held this secret close in her heart. She would reveal it to everyone once she passed the LSAT and receive the admission letter from the USC School of Law.

Later that evening, Zina was making cheese enchiladas and discovered she had no enchilada sauce. She scooped up Miles and made her way over to Juan Carlos' apartment. He was home; she heard music playing softly in the background. She tapped on his door, and Miles started to bark.

Juan Carlos opened the door, his face flushed, holding a wine glass and smiling.

"Hey, chica!"

"Sorry to intrude, but I'm making enchiladas and don't have any enchilada sauce. Do you have any?"

He ushered her in with a raised eyebrow.

"That devil you call a dog must remain in your arms!

Can't have him upsetting Ms. Kitty."

Zina laughed and held onto him a little tighter as she entered his living room. She saw a Hispanic man on the couch, dark hair with scattered teeth like a white picket fence. He had a streetwise appearance. Juan Carlos waved his hand.

"Oh, Zina meet Ricardo, my friend."

"Hello, Ricardo" she said, extending a manicured hand. "Hello."

He stood up. He was short, with beautiful brown eyes and a short haircut. He was not handsome, just ordinary looking. Zina knew he was just filling up the empty lonely spaces and places within Juan Carlos, though he was a poor substitute for Giovanni.

"Your dog is cute," he said in broken English.

"Thank you."

She followed Juan Carlos to the kitchen. Juan Carlos went into his fully stocked pantry to retrieve a can of red Enchilada sauce and handed it to her.

Ms. Kitty was in the kitchen witnessing the transaction. Miles was getting anxious in her arms.

"Fabulous, you are a lifesaver. Would you and your friend like to join me for enchiladas?"

"Thanks, but we are going to order in, maybe

Mediterranean tonight," he said with a devilish grin.

Zina picked up the hint and scurried back over to her apartment. It was had been twenty Saturdays since her mother passed away and sadness enveloped her heart. God, she missed her. She recalled the delicious peach cobblers, her giggle, her smiling eyes and quick wit. Her mother was her everything, and her death left a huge void. Zina felt disconnected. She went through all the motions, but there was an emptiness within her soul. Donovan was supportive and loving, but it was not enough.

Zina recalled the trips to visit their cousins in Gary, Indiana, and how her parents would stop at White Castle and load up on burgers and cheeseburgers. She also recalled living on Drexel as a child playing in the dirt with her friends. She remembered her first kiss under the L.

Chicago held so many memories in her heart. It was home but she no longer felt safe there, so she had made the decision to relocate to Los Angeles to start life over again. Her family was shocked; her mother did not want her to leave, but she understood why she had to leave Chicago. She did not press the issue or try to change her mind.

Chicago was her lifeblood, the windy city. She missed the magnificent skyline, Lake Shore Drive, Sears Tower. It was a beautiful city, forever etched into the fabric of her childhood. But today, her life is different without her mother. Her mother's absence felt strange and cruel, but life continued to move forward without Maxine in it. Did not the world realize she was missing? How could the world continue to move, people hurrying in an out of traffic without a care? Did not they realize Zina was in pain, her mother was no longer living? How could life be so cold? The world was less sweet without her beloved mother.

Chapter 27

"How's Daddy?" Zina asked Marlo.

"He is just existing, sitting in his favorite chair staring out of the window. I believe he has not wrapped his mind around her absence." Zina could relate. She felt like she was living outside of herself.

Existing...what an appropriate word. Numb. Her life was numb, without feeling. She was just existing. What a life! She was just taking little bites out of her life, living her life in increments, small doses at a time. That's all she could manage. Emotionally, she could not take in her entire life. It was too much for her to bear. Another tragedy had robbed her of what little joy remained. Her mother's death was like a punch in the gut.

Tears welled up in her soft brown eyes. She cried all the time, in the dark in her apartment, alone. Miles probably wondered what was wrong with her. He'd sit staring at her, tongue hanging out of his mouth, wanting some love and affection. That she could handle, loving her little doggie.

Meanwhile, Donovan took out a five million dollar life insurance policy listing Zina as the sole beneficiary. He was planning on doing something good with the money, clean it up, as well as his guilty conscience. He was in deep and wanted a way out of this situation. He thought long and hard about it and came up with a brilliant plan. He felt the Russians were going to kill Zina because they assumed she knew about the blackmail attempts with Troy, although she didn't. Zina had disclosed a few pieces of information about her and Troy's relationship, but Donovan was positive she knew nothing about the Russian involvement. Troy had kept that hidden to protect her; however, he was the sacrifice.

Donovan and the Russians had Zina and her family under surveillance at the funerals for Troy and Nina. Zina never disclosed to anyone that her sister was alive—not a soul. The family was instructed to keep the secret, because Nina's life depended on it. As far as the Russians were concerned, she was deceased. But they discovered Zina was her twin.

Donovan was a double spy. He had Zina under surveillance for the Russians, but he did not count on falling in love with her. He was torn, but he had devised a plan to ease his guilt.

Zina had not heard from Troy's beloved sister Bailey in a while.

She was surprised at the phone call.

"Hey, lady!"

"Bailey! How are you and the family?"

"We're fine, just wrapping up the annual fundraiser."

"Great. Troy would have been so proud."

Zina's heart sank at the mention of his name.

"The reason I'm calling, love, is to invite you out to the fundraiser next month."

Zina hesitated.

"Um, that's wonderful. What date?"

Then Bailey remembered Zina was in Chicago a few months earlier for her mother's funeral.

"Love, I'm sorry. I just recalled you were home recently for Mother Maxine's homegoing. Don't mean to be insensitive. Please forgive me."

Zina appreciated the comment.

"Thank you, sweetie, it's okay."

"It's on the 10th. Let me know if you can make it. I would love to spend some time with you. The family misses and love you dearly. You are still a big part of our lives, and it don't matter if you living in Los Angeles."

Zina's heart was touched by her words. The thought of returning to Chicago again drained her. It was too soon after her mother's death. But she did need to spend some time with her father and siblings. Memories flooded her mind once again as she thought about her beloved city. She missed the smell and taste of Chicago, Illinois. The spectacular change of seasons, the orange and red leaves, the white Christmas every year, the humidity in the summer as they sunbathed on the beach. Her heart smiled as the thoughts took her to the familiar lovely places that framed her life. She let out a sigh. It would be good to spend some time with her dad. Maybe a visit from her would cheer him up a bit.

Zina thought about the Troy Blackwell Foundation and was touched his family extending an invitation to her. She pulled out her laptop and searched for the website. It was awesome. The images were sharp, clear, and they had a section entitled Troy's Page which detailed his vision as well as the legacy he left. Tears formed as she closed her Apple laptop.

Donovan interrupted via FaceTime. He looked good. "Hey, baby."

"Hey, how are you?" she asked.

"I'm good; how are you, Z?"

"Sleepy, but I'm fine. Considering going home next month for the fundraiser for Troy's foundation. His people called and invited me."

"That's cool. So, they are carrying on his work in the community?"

"Yes. Troy loved working with at-risk youth. It was his passion."

Donovan realized it was really a rarity for her to discuss Troy with him. She never did, but he welcomed it. Zina realized she may have said too much, and decided to change the subject.

"How's the tour going? What city are you in?"

"The tour is great. We're in Seattle and its' raining cats and dogs. Seattle is a beautiful city, though."

"Okay, where to next?"

"Portland. So, baby, I was thinking when I return from the tour, I want to take you away for a couple weeks."

"Really? Where to?"

"I want to surprise you. Are you down?"

Zina thought about it briefly, and gave into the moment. "Sure," she giggled.

Donovan blew her a kiss. "Love and miss you, baby."

She smiled.

"I miss and love you, too"

After Zina hung up, Donovan did a search and came across the Troy Blackwell Foundation website. He read a few of the pages. He discovered the page for making donations and decided to make a million dollar donation, anonymously, of course. He followed the prompts and when he hit send, he felt a chill go up his spine.

Chapter 28

lthough he did not pull the trigger in the assassination of Troy, he shot Nina. He was in the SUV that night waiting and watching. The guilt ate away at him. Zina was the target of the Russians' surveillance. Donovan was a double-spy, not only for the Russians, but also for the FBI. Donating this money was his way of easing his guilt. After his assignment with Zina was complete, he would disappear just as easily as he had entered her life. His exit would be just as quick.

He felt bad. She would be shocked not knowing why he left, but he had to do it. His life depended on it. His entire life was a lie. Everything he disclosed to Zina was a lie. It was all to deceive her in order to find out if she knew about the Russian mafia and their ties to Troy Blackwell. The FBI was investigating the Russian mafia money laundering operation in the Chicago area. It was a huge and lucrative money laundering operation and the FBI was closing in on the entire mafia organization. Chicago was the main city; however, the mafia had ties in other major cities as well.

It was bigger than Donovan. This was an international operation that had been in place in the United States for several years. They were able to come in under the radar through local communities that were oppressed, such as the Hispanic and African- American communities. It was a well-planned and executed operation.

Juan Carlos knocked on her door loudly, startling Zina.

"Why you knocking on my door like that?" she asked, opening the door.

He was somewhat disheveled and his face was flushed. "Girl, my private investigator got a lead on that snake, Giovanni!" he said with excitement in his voice.

Zina ran her hands through her curly fro.

"Really? Do tell!"

Juan Carlos had Ms. Kitty tucked neatly in his forearm and plopped himself down on her loveseat.

"It appears that dirty snake is in South Beach, Florida. He opened up a salon in a very upscale area. The funding for it is well-hidden, but I told the P.I. to keep digging," he said in an angry tone. "I'm sure he's gone through that money I loaned him!"

Juan Carlos was red. He was excited about getting to the bottom of this scandal.

"I can't wait to take him to court to try to recover some of the funds. He must be out of his pea brain if he thinks he can just take my money and run!"

Zina provided the listening ear his mood called for. Juan Carlos continued to ramble on and on about Giovanni and seeking justice. He was right, and Zina felt bad for him, but he should have seen it coming. Giovanni was a hustler and it was written all over him. She only hoped this would teach Juan Carlos a lesson.

Clearing her throat, she asked

"How is Ricardo?"

"He's okay," he answered, rolling his eyes. "He was over last night. He's getting on my very last nerve, girlfriend. Too clingy! He's a Cancer, whew!"

The guy with the scattered teeth was only temporarily filling an emptiness in Juan Carlos' life. No one could fill that hole in his soul. *Only therapy.*

Chapter 29

"She had to be moved to an undisclosed location," Marlo explained.

"What happened, LoLo?" Zina asked

"I can't really get into the details I'm at work, but she is alive and had to be moved to a location that even we cannot know about."

"That is serious!" Zina voiced started to crack.

"We are devastated. Pops is going to move in with us for the time being."

"This is unreal!"

"Yes, but I have to go to roll call. We'll chat soon. I have to get another phone, a burner. I'll be in touch...love you."

Zina could not believe the Russians had discovered her sister was alive. She had not told one soul about her twin—not Donovan, Desiree... The Russians had to have her parents' home under electronic surveillance. She may have mentioned it to Juan Carlos when she first moved in. Zina recalls drinking and chatting one night with him, but how could that conversation have been discovered? It was so long ago, it did not make sense. She wondered if her house was bugged. Paranoia began to set in.

Zina realized she would not see her twin for a while, and this unnerved her to no end. As usual, she reached for her stash and went to the kitchen for a glass of wine. The moment called for it, but she knew it was just a temporary fix. She could not disclose this to anyone. After all, her sister's life was at stake and she could not bear to risk her twin's life. Perhaps she would get more answers when Marlo called her back. Until then, she was on pins and needles; her nerves were frayed.

"Marlo's next call was very brief. Get a new phone today!" she ordered.

"Why?" Zina asked.

"Can't discuss that until you get rid of that phone." she answered, and abruptly hung up.

Zina was pissed because of the inconvenience, but it was necessary. She purchased a new cell phone and immediately called her sister.

"Okay, what is going on with my phone?" she asked Marlo.

"Your phone has been compromised!" she responded.

Zina was silent trying to process this news.

"How did you determine that?"

"Chicago Police Department has been tracking your personal cell phone and discovered some strange issues which I'm not at liberty to discuss," she said matter-of-factly. This only confused Zina even more.

"Who is behind this?" Zina asked.

"We're not sure; still looking into it. Whoever is behind it is very sophisticated; the technology is cutting edge."

"Who the hell could it be?" Zina had no clue.

"Well, it's someone in your inner circle because of the technology used. That's all I can say, sis."

Zina knew not to press the issue any further. She was confused and afraid at the same time, wondering who it could be.

Zina was engrossed in billing on her Apple laptop when she received a Facetime from Donovan.

"Hey, baby, what's up? Tried calling you..."

"Hey, had to change my number. It's kinda crazy. An old boyfriend was stalking me and got my number. Sorry I did not tell you; didn't want to worry you," she lied.

Donovan seemed to accept the lie, but had questions.

"Should I be concerned? Is he violent? Did he show up at your house? Has he made any threats?"

"No, nothing like that. He's just tripping," Zina continued the lie, being evasive.

"What did he do, Z?"

Zina had to brush him off quickly.

"Nothing, babe. It's okay. Just some stupid social media stuff, but the matter has been resolved."

"You want me to handle this? I will protect you. All you have to do is say the word, I got you."

"Absolutely not! Let it go! I have a new number. I'm good!

Thanks, babe."

She sensed he was slightly irritated.

"I appreciate your concern. I didn't mean to keep it from you. I just thought it was petty. Didn't want to bother you."

"Your safety and well-being are not petty; it's too many nut jobs out there and I need to know...if you have any problems, come to me. Got it?"

"Yes," she said through a sly smile.

Chapter 30

The next morning, Marlo told Zina where Nina was.

"She was relocated to Lovejoy, Georgia," Marlo whispered into the telephone.

"So this means we cannot have any contact with her whatsoever?" Zina inquired.

"Yes, that's correct."

"For how long?"

"Not sure."

"This is very troubling. How are we supposed to deal with this? After all, she is my twin and she is going to be disconnected from everyone who loves her!"

Zina was furious. Marlo attempted to calm her down. "But it's necessary for her safety."

Zina let out a heavy sigh. The weight of this problem was very heavy.

In the meantime, guilt had been eating away at Donovan. He had shot and—he thought—killed his woman's twin sister. The Russian Mafia thought she was dead, until they overheard the telephone calls indicating otherwise. He was shocked. Zina never mentioned she had a twin sister, Nina, whom he had assumed was dead. He thought she was an employee, never made the connection.

Donovan recalled the Chicago Tribune publishing the murders. They indicated the woman killed was an employee of the agency. The Russian mafia had surveillance at both funerals; Donovan was assigned to Zina. Nina had been placed in protective custody because of the Russian mafia. Donovan was in deep with them, and being a double spy was extremely dangerous. As soon as they discovered Nina was alive, a hit was ordered; however, the attempt was aborted. The witness protection moved her the day of the plot to assassinate Nina.

Donovan was suspicious about Zina's phone number being changed. He knew it was related to her sister. It was also obvious Zina and her family were very guarded about her phone being compromised.

Zina's heart was heavy again, feeling like she had experienced another death. No contact with her twin for God knows how long. Feeling helpless, she wanted to scream.

Instead, she reached for her crutch, weed. She fired up the blunt, took a deep hit, and slowly blew out the smoke. The marijuana filled her body and head, and after a few minutes she was emotionally numb. She closed her eyes and laid her head on the soft pillow.

Miles decided he wanted some attention and jumped up on the sofa to join her. He licked her hand. She opened her eyes, smiled and started petting him. He moved closer. Her little furry companion sweetened her mood. She was grateful for this canine gift from Juan Carlos.

Zina wondered what happened to her yesterday. How could she move in today and tomorrow? She was weary. She felt as if her family was slowly slipping away from her. Her mother's passing hurt her to the core of her being, and now her Father was just existing, a shell of the man he once was. Her twin sister was in the south and they were unsure about when and how to contact her because she had been discovered.

Things became real, and Zina increased her marijuana usage. Numbing her pain was her only coping mechanism, at least for the time being. Her relationship with Donovan was suspect and she was watching him with a side-eye. Was he the one who bugged her cell phone? She did not want to believe he was capable of such a deed. But who else could it be?

Donovan was also tired of living a double life. He wanted to wrap it up and get ghost on Zina. He was too emotionally invested and it was weighing him down. He hoped she would never discover it was he who shot her twin. He would be returning to Los Angeles soon, and he had to come up with a plan to leave Zina for good.

The Russian mafia had no clue as to Nina's new location. Since all the telephone numbers had been changed, they had no way to determine her whereabouts. The FBI was closing in on the mafia after years of investigating the crime ring.

Several Chicago businesses were willing to testify to the grand jury. The FBI still had them under surveillance and had enough evidence to issue indictments all the way to the top.

"I can't believe it's been a week since I had a blunt," Zina stated.

"I'm so proud of you, and glad you made an appointment with Dr. Sylvia. You're going to love her. She will help you deal with the grief, addiction, and any other issues," Desiree assured Zina.

"She's that good?"

"Trust."

Zina released a heavy sigh from her soul, she was not

feeling therapy at all.

Desiree felt it.

"Girl, this is something you should have dealt with a long time ago. Losing Troy so tragically and almost losing your twin. Not to mention your beloved Mother. So much tragedy within a few years. You've kept all this bottled up inside, which is unhealthy, and the very issues we run away from are exactly what we need to confront."

Zina nodded her head in agreement, but still felt uneasy about discussing her problems with a complete stranger.

"I'm still uncomfortable with it, D. I mean, I appreciate the referral, but I'm scared."

Desiree touched her hand.

"I understand, Zina, but you are going to be fine. You must trust the process."

Zina was still feeling a certain kind of way about this therapy business. She gave her friend her word, but was not looking forward to next week with Dr. Sylvia. In the meantime, she was watching Donovan like a hawk. Mistrust sat in her belly as she was very guarded around him. This was new and funky. She hated this space. Uncertainty. Being suspicious of the man she shared a life with.

Damn, she wanted a blunt and glass of wine. However,

she was not smoking weed or drinking liquor. Being disconnected from her twin was the catalyst that woke her up. Reality was no joke. Now she was wide awake, and did not like the hand life had dealt her.

Dr. Sylvia had a lovely inviting office which was surprising given the fact that it was near Beverly Hills. Dr. Sylvia was a beautiful brown-skinned statuesque woman with a warm smile and kind eyes. Her voice was like silk, smooth and calming. Zina liked her instantly. She felt a connection to this woman; it was weird. Dr. Sylvia invited Zina in. Her office wall was sprinkled with her various credentials and awards mixed with a few pictures, but not in a pretentious manner. She appeared to be grounded, friendly with a strong sense of who she was without apology.

"Tell me why you decided to undergo therapy," she asked.

Zina cleared her throat. This lady got straight to the point. She began the difficult journey of uncovering her grief and pain. Dr. Sylvia listened intently without interruption while taking notes.

"I just want to commend you for taking the first step to bring about healing, because nothing covered up gets healed. We at times reach outside of ourselves to numb our emotions with alcohol, drugs, sex, gambling, and various other elements in order to put a Band-Aid on our wounds."

This made perfect sense to Zina. *She is good!*

Dr. Sylvia continued.

"I want to explain to you the five stages of grief, which are denial, anger, bargaining, depression, and acceptance. Some people may experience all of the stages while others may undergo two stages rather than five; however, these five stages of grief are the most commonly observed. Let's examine the symptoms of grief for just a moment. Can you explain some of the issues you've experienced these past few months?"

Zina took a deep breath and told her, "I've been feeling detached, I cry a lot alone in the dark when no one is around, I have sleepless nights, and sometimes I feel like my life has no purpose."

Dr. Sylvia continued with her notetaking.

"Thank you for your honesty. I'm glad you feel comfortable uncovering the layers of pain and grief that you've experienced. We will take this journey together. Remember, this process cannot be rushed. Healing takes time. I will give you a few exercises to assist you in this journey. How does that sound?"

"Fine, not a problem."

"Okay, that's good. Now, how does it feel?"

Zina felt like Dr. Sylvia pierced her soul with this question. She did not want to feel anything right now, and was experiencing a little anxiety. A lone tear began to make a track down her face.

"Scary," was all she could muster.

"Good. That's a great place to start, fear! Why are you fearful, Zina?"

"Because I'm not accustomed to feeling anything without smoking a blunt or drinking alcohol. I've been avoiding my feelings for a while, and now I have nothing to lean on to help me not feel."

"Wow, that's honest and real! You are on the right track in confronting your feelings without the crutches of alcohol and weed. I'm proud of you."

Zina felt her soul explode with joy. The therapy session went better than she expected and her load felt a little lighter today. She looked forward to her next appointment with Dr. Sylvia. In the meantime, she had several legal documents to file. It seems her work got busier; however, she had a part-time assistant who was efficient and productive.

Zina's life appeared to be heading in a more positive direction.

However, not being in contact with her twin Nina continued to shake her to the core and she was having a difficult time processing it. Marlo informed her that whoever inserted the tracking device in her cell phone was very clever and it almost went undetected.

No communication with her twin and suspecting Donovan of planting that device in her phone were the catalysts to propel her into therapy. It was too much for her to handle, and she was at the end of her mental rope. Besides, it was too soon after the death of her beloved Mother to deal with any more heartbreaking news. It seemed like it was one crisis after another as of late and she was tired; emotionally drained with all these recent events. Going to therapy was a way for her to not only process her feelings, but to get out of her own head. At times, she felt like her head was going to explode with all the crap she was currently dealing with.

Zina felt good as she entered her apartment. Miles ran to greet her, and she petted her pooch.

"Hey, Miles!" "

His tail wagged with excitement as he licked her hand. She continued to lavish him with attention. The familiar knock of the door startled her. She got up to answer.

"Whew, have I got some tea for you! Could not wait for

you to get home!" Juan Carlos stated, his face slightly red.

"Hello to you, too!"

"Hello," he said, plopping himself down on her sofa.

"Sorry, I'm just about to explode with this news!" he exclaimed, fanning himself. He had left Ms. Kitty at home, which was shocking. He very rarely did that.

"What's up?" Zina asked.

"That snake in the grass, Giovanni, has been arrested and he is in custody!" he said smiling.

"What? Do tell!"

"It appears he got involved with a very wealthy man and attempted to blackmail him. Well, turns out this man was not only in the closet but well-connected politically and his brother is the State Attorney in Florida. Talk about karma! Could not happen to a better person! That slimy dog is finally getting his justice!"

Juan Carlos was excited.

"Good! I'm just disappointed you cannot recoup your money. Nonetheless, he won't be able to take advantage of anyone else."

"Anyhoo, what's for dinner, chica?" Zina rolled her eyes.

"I'm going to order - how does California Pizza Kitchen sound?"

"Fabulous!"

The following day, Zina had a late appointment and had to make her way to Studio City to meet with a client. She was in a hurry as she walked at a fast pace to her Black BMW X3. She clicked her car alarm and slid into the camel-colored leather driver's seat. She loved her whip. It had tinted windows and a state-of-the art stereo system. Closing her door, a strange uneasy feeling suddenly came upon her that she could not shake. She started the ignition, checked her mirror, and all of a sudden the familiar face in the rearview mirror frightened her. She jumped.

"Donovan!"

He gazed at her with a bizarre look on his face that made her uneasy. All of a sudden her passenger door opened and a strange looking white man slid into the front seat. He had a silver metal gun with a silencer on it. Zina swallowed hard as confusion enveloped her. Why was Donovan staring at her with such intensity? Why didn't Donovan say anything to the stranger who slid into her car? Where did he come from? Why was he looking at her the same way Donovan was? What was Donovan doing in the back seat? Who the hell was this man with the gun? What did he want with her?

The strange man started speaking a foreign language to

Donovan and what was shocking was that he was speaking back to him fluently. What in the hell was going on? Zina was speechless. She looked back and forth at them as they continued to converse. All of a sudden, the man handed the gun to Donovan, who pointed it in Zina's direction. She was shocked and speechless. There was complete silence, then Bang!

www.ingramcontent.com/pod-product-compliance
Lightning Source LLC
Chambersburg PA
CBHW070928250626
47159CB00009B/3166